Nobody ever thought that the Hole
in the Wall Gang would attempt to
rob Hopewell's town bank; they didn't
believe the Stillwell Mob would try it
either, let alone the ageing Hash Knife
Gang, as the Bank was the most solid
building in the whole of the
ramshackle town – it had walls a foot
thick, only one entrance and a big
sturdy vault – but they did!

The trouble started when the local
newspaper printed a long article on
how the sheriff, Adam Bricker, had
been seen making apple dumplings
for a family of five deserted children
while the midnight special was being
held up by the Stillwell Mob. It
seemed the outlaws decided that a
man who is busy making apple
dumplings wouldn't have much time
for law and order and that's where
they made their mistake, for when all
three gangs attack the same bank at
the same time Sheriff Bricker proves
to the town that a good cook can also
be a mighty dangerous lawman!

Jack M. Bickham

The
Apple Dumpling Gang

CORGI BOOKS
A DIVISION OF TRANSWORLD PUBLISHERS LTD

THE APPLE DUMPLING GANG

A CORGI/CAROUSEL BOOK 0 552 09857 4

Originally published in Great Britain
by Robert Hale & Co. Ltd.

PRINTING HISTORY
Robert Hale edition published 1972
Corgi/Carousel edition published 1975
Corgi/Carousel edition reprinted 1975

Copyright © 1971 by Jack M. Bickham

This low-priced Corgi Book has been completely
reset in a type face designed for easy reading,
and was printed from new plates. It contains
the complete text of the original hard-cover
edition.

Corgi Books are published by
Transworld Publishers Ltd.,
Cavendish House, 57–59 Uxbridge Road,
Ealing, London W.5.
Made and printed in Great Britain by
Cox & Wyman Ltd., London, Reading and Fakenham

Chapter One

The fact that John Wintle was drunk didn't matter.

'It doesn't matter,' Bricker said patiently. 'You cause no trouble, you can stay drunk all you want. You know that. You know how we operate the law in this town.'

'Yeah,' Wintle sobbed, tears appearing in his blood-shot eyes.

Bricker sighed and took his booted feet down off his desk. He leaned his elbows forward into the pile of old wanted posters, playing cards, mummified fruit peels and unanswered correspondence on the work surface. 'What do you want, John?'

Wintle fished in the front pocket of his overalls. 'I got me a ticket on the train. I'm going to San Francisco.'

'When?' Bricker asked.

'Tonight. Right away.'

Bricker thought about this. In a town like Hopewell, a habitual drunk like John Wintle was a minor annoyance. Still, if Wintle was getting out, it was a tiny relief.

'This is sudden, isn't it?' he asked. 'You've quit your job at the store?'

'Yep. Sort of.'

You mean,' Bricker said, 'you got fired

'Yep,' Wintle admitted. 'But I got to make this trip anyhow.'

'What do you want me to do? Pour you on the train?'

'Well, I got a, uh, shipment coming in on the stage tomorrow. But I've got to leave tonight, you see? So I wondered, could you meet the stage and claim my shipment and take care of it for me.'

Bricker leaned back in his battered swivel chair. 'What is this shipment?'

'Valuables,' Wintle said, avoiding his eyes.

'All right, John,' Bricker snapped. 'I'll pick up your package. Whatever it is, I'll pick it up and stow it here in the jailhouse for you. When do you plan to be back from San Francisco?'

'I don't know,' Wintle said evasively. 'Aw, Sheriff, you're a good man and I'm no good, I know that—'

'I'll keep the package,' Bricker cut in, 'until you do get back. Whenever that is. All right?'

Wintle began crying. 'Oh, thank you, Sheriff. You're a good man, and I'm going to mend my ways. I know I'm no good, but I'm going to be better, I'm going to stop drinking—'

'*Out!*' Bricker bellowed, going to the wall in self-defence.

Bricker had moved to Hopewell right after the war between the States. Even then the town hadn't been much. Back before the war, a cattle trail went through the area, but other trails soon proved better and the Hopewell route was abandoned. There had been a mission for the Indians here once, too, but most of the Indians moved farther west. There had been some good springs in the surrounding hills and mesa country, but they had gone dry, mostly, so the railroad didn't do much business and the only thing that kept the rails from getting rusty was traffic going through, going to better places. Never very prosperous, Hopewell had been going downhill for a long time, and sometimes people wondered how far it was to absolute, rock bottom. They had been wondering when Bricker arrived right after the war, and they were still wondering, fifteen years later.

He had gotten a job as deputy to the sheriff, met and fell in love with a girl, got married, stayed, became sheriff in a special election after his boss got killed and he then rounded up the killers. Then in what seemed a very short time, his wife got a slight fever which became a worse fever which became the smallpox and then she died.

It was a miserable job in a miserable place. Hopewell had about two thousand people in it: dirt farmers, drifters, small-time cattlemen, merchants, gamblers, whores, clerks, thieves, bartenders, cooks, butchers, judges, preachers, drummers, wives, and children.

The town itself was located in a long dirt flat with broken badlands—woods and gullies and rolling hills— off to the east, and broken-rock mountains off on the horizon to the west. To the south a mile or so was a long, rounded, ham-shaped mesa, so it was called Ham Mesa. To the north a mile or so was another landmark, a sharply peaked knob of rock called Tightwad Hill. Nobody knew why.

People said Bricker was fearless, which was a damned lie, of course. They also said he was a hard, fair man. He had been sheriff a long time. He didn't care for it much, but it was a living. He lived in a small house he had built onto the back of the building where the office and the jail were. He had some friends with whom he played nickel-dime poker, a lot of nodding acquaintances, and enough of a reputation that the really serious outlaws didn't come right into Hopewell much, preferring to hole up in the surrounding countryside which was so rough that an army couldn't have flushed them. Nevertheless, the fact that the outlaws were *in the vicinity* had in recent months provided grist for the Hopewell newspaper, which was trying to build its circulation with a small campaign against Bricker.

About six o'clock, Bricker left his jailhouse office and limped up the street into the teeth of the dying sun. The frame and 'dobe buildings along Main Street's twisted length cast long, grotesque shadows. Bricker walked to the depot. Inside the echoing brick shed, the ticket agent sat behind a wicket reading the latest copy of the *Hopewell Record*.

At a baggage wagon heaped with packages, a bald, fat storekeeper sweated and mumbled as he shoved parcels around, separating those that had been unloaded for him. The storekeeper hefted a keg of nails off the wagon and sat it down heavily. The keg had stencilled on the side FODY DRYGOODS, HOPE-WELL, JARVIS FODY, PROP.

'Evening, Jarvis. Evening, Mayor.' Bricker said as another man approached.

Mayor Oliver Steed patted daintily at his face with a

lace handkerchief. 'Good evening, Sheriff. Are you expecting a shipment on the train?'

Bricker hiked a foot up on the wagon. 'Nope. Just wondered if John Wintle got on it all right.'

'He got on it,' Fody grunted, wrestling a box, 'but they almost needed a funnel to pour him on with.'

'Will we be playing poker tonight?' Bricker asked.

'I'm willing. Might be a mite late, with this unloading to do.'

The mayor dabbed at his nostrils with the linen. 'I'm surprised you're in a mood for amusement tonight, Sheriff.'

'Why do you say that?' Bricker asked, puzzled.

'After the editorial in today's *Record*.'

Fody straightened up from his packages. 'It's a humdinger, Adam. I thought you'd have heard. I guess everybody was afraid that short fuse of yours would be burned all the way down, and they didn't want to get in your way.'

Bricker recalled that the afternoon had been unusually quiet, especially in the vicinity of his office. He had been dozing when Wintle staggered in. This explained it.

'Will you still want to play poker tonight?'

'How do I know?' Bricker roared over his shoulder. 'Of course! Why not?' Fuming, he headed for the *Record* office.

Three or four men stood out in front of the frame building that housed the newspaper, reading copies of the latest edition. They spotted Bricker coming, and scattered like quail. Bricker tromped up the steps and went into the building. There was a counter in the front, and behind it the typecases and press and machinery and desks. Mrs Enright, a pretty redhead, started forward to wait on Bricker, then recognized him. She scattered like quail, too.

Harold Enright walked up from the back. Tall and slender, and looking younger than his thirty-five years, he had dark curly hair and a boyish face. He wore a smudged printer's apron over his white shirt and black trousers. He was smiling.

'Hello, Sheriff. What can we do for you?'

Bricker tossed his pennies on the counter. 'I want a copy of the paper.'

Enright grinned. 'My pleasure.' He dug a copy out from under the counter and handed it over.

Bricker glared at the front page. He didn't have to look any further. The editorial was set two columns wide and ran right at the top.

BRICKER MUST GO

The *Record* is second to none in its admiration for the fine record posted over the many years by this community's distinguished senior lawman, Adam Bricker. But every indicator now tells us that Father Time has moved his inexorable way, and it is far past the time for Adam Bricker to resign and let a young man take over.

It is our civic duty to make the facts clear as we see them.

Adam Bricker has been a brave and fine defender of law and order. He has been our sheriff for fifteen years. In that time, he has performed notably in apprehending the infamous Cody gang a decade ago, in arresting

Billy Slade and his accomplices five years ago, and in bringing to justice countless lesser criminals.

Bricker's many friends point to these exploits in defending him today. But the truth is that he can no longer be defended. Look at the facts.

The Stillwell Mob is reported on good authority to be operating within a 50-mile radius of our fair community. The Hole in the Wall Gang continues to operate out of the general vicinity, and the sheriff is unable to find these outlaws. The Hash Knife Outfit robbed a Frisco train less than one hundred miles from here a week ago, and lawmen said the thieves were tracked into the Hopewell area.

In addition, scarcely a night passes without a violent robbery, a homicide, a theft or some other breach of the peace. The tempo of lawlessness grows worse. It must be stopped!

If Adam Bricker loves this community, and if he loves law and order, he will serve both by resigning promptly. Each day's new violence and bloodshed proves that he is no longer capable of defending justice. We call on him to step down.

Bricker finished reading the editorial with an odd heavy spot in the bottom of his stomach. He read parts again, the parts, especially, about him being too old.

Harold Enright was standing there with his hands lightly on the counter, watching him. Bricker looked up at him. Enright had the same slight smile, but he looked pale.

'Why?' Bricker asked.

'A newspaper has a responsibility—'

'You're young, Harold, especially in the number of years you've been out in this country. But you ain't stupid. You know better than this.'

Enright's face coloured. 'I believe every word of that.'

'These gangs don't come to Hopewell.'

'They might.'

'They *don't*. And you know what kind of "violence" and "robbery" and "homicide" we've been having around here: a drunk fighting a drunk; two kids breaking into the dry-goods; a knife fight between two drifters no one had ever seen around town before that night.'

Enright's pinched face became pale again, but he stuck to his guns. 'It's getting worse all the time. I admire you personally and I'm sorry, but—'

A gunshot exploded outside, and a woman screamed.

Bricker ran outside and immediately spotted the commotion a half block up the street to his right. It wasn't hard to read. A wagon stood in front of a small store with some supplies stacked on the tailgate. Out in the street were four people: a young wife cringing against the side of the wagon, her dress torn off one shoulder; a youthful towheaded waddie holding her by one arm; another young, lanky rider-type with a gun in his hand, and a man dressed in farmer togs sprawled in the dust. A few spectators stood around, but well back against the building, scared and staying out of it.

Bricker ran. As he did so, he saw that the shot must have gone wild because the farmer in the street was not dead, was struggling to get to his feet. The lanky youth with a gun in his hand stepped forward and clipped the victim neatly on the side of the head. The man sprawled unconscious and the woman, hysterical, screamed again. The youth holding her arm twisted it.

'What's going on?' Bricker bawled, striding up.

The towhead whirled to face him, still hanging onto the farm wife, who was youthful and pretty. Bricker recognized her and remembered the name, Clayborne; lived east of town. She looked terrified, and her ordinarily bright—possibly saucy—eyes were glazed.

'No problem,' the towhead said, taking in Bricker, the gun and the badge on the vest all simultaneously.

The other youth also turned to face Bricker, although he remained farther into the street, near his unconscious victim. 'That's right, Sheriff. Just a little argument.'

'It looks like more,' Bricker said. 'Both of you put down your guns. You. Let go of her.'

'This is a private deal,' the towhead growled. He had been drinking.

Bricker felt sweat on his back. The towhead was just drunk enough to be ugly. Where the hell was Billy Dean? What good was it having a deputy if he was never around at times like this?

Bricker tried to play it close. 'Your name's Johnson, isn't it?'

The towhead nodded pugnaciously.

'And you're Selvie,' Bricker identified the other one.

'It's a private deal,' Johnson said, still hanging onto the woman.

'And I said you'd better let her go,' Bricker repeated.

'We're good enough to flirt with and kid along,' Johnson shot back, 'but then when her old man is along, she gives us the cold shoulder. No woman does that to me!'

A few more people had run to join the crowd, but they were all staying well back, silent, watchful. With his peripheral vision, Bricker saw the newspaperman, Enright, in the group farthest back. Bricker felt his anger rising. He didn't want to have gunplay. He might not be able to avoid it. But as usual, no one was breaking his back to step forward to help. Having Enright among the silent spectators was worst of all.

But there was hardly time to think about that now. The towhead, Johnson, was glaring at him, waiting a move. The other youth, Selvie, seemed sober, but committed. Selvie might be more dangerous, but Johnson would be the one to hair-trigger violence.

Bricker assumed a conciliatory attitude. It galled him. 'You boys put your guns down. There's no need for bad trouble here. I want to know exactly what happened. But even before that, let her go and put down the guns.'

Johnson hung onto the woman, who was wincing with the pain of his grip. Selvie retained his Colt in hand although it was at his side.

Johnson flared, 'It's private, I told you!'

'I'm asking you,' Bricker said evenly.

'She flirted with us, then when we got friendly today, her old man was along, so she told him we was causing trouble. He started it!'

Behind the two men, a figure appeared out of the crowd. Tall, lantern-jawed, slow-moving, almost sleepy in his attitude. Bricker felt a pulse of relief. It was his deputy.

The two men had their backs turned to Dean's approach, however, and knew nothing. Dean moved nearer, closing behind them. Slowly he drew his gun.

'Let the woman go,' Bricker told Johnson.

'You go to hell,' Johnson fired back. 'Don't mess in this, I'm warning you! We're two to your one! I'll fight you if I have to!'

'You don't want to do that,' Bricker said.

'I will I'll fight you! You don't scare me!'

Dean crept closer, moving behind Johnson, ten feet behind him.

'Last chance,' Bricker said flatly.

'You'll die,' Johnson said, his eyes getting wild. 'You're old, man. You're *old*. You were good once, but we'll kill you! I'm warning you, leave us be!'

Bricker looked at Selvie. 'My deputy is right behind him. He'll never clear leather with his iron. If you try to raise that piece in your hand, you're a dead man.'

Johnson giggled shrilly. 'Somebody behind me, huh! Somebody's behind me, Sel,' he added with heavy sarcasm. 'The oldest trick in the book, and this poor old man tries it on us. Do you think we're stupid, old man? Do you think we'll turn so you can gun us?'

Behind him, Billy Dean raised his gun and brought it down sharply, right on top of Johnson's head. The *clunk!* was loud, and Johnson went down like a felled tree.

Selvie panicked and started to raise his gun.

'*Don't!*' Bricker snapped.

Selvie froze.

Billy Dean hustled over and took the gun from his hand.

The woman began sobbing uncontrollably as she knelt beside her husband.

Billy Dean grinned proudly at Bricker. 'I got 'em, boy! I snuck up, just like an Injun, heh?'

'Take charge of the prisoners,' Bricker suggested.

Dean scurried, businesslike.

Going to the woman and her husband, Bricker ascertained that he wasn't badly hurt. The crowd pressed around, much too close. Bricker got to his feet. 'Everybody get back!'

Enright refused to budge. 'How about a statement, Sheriff?'

'Die,' Bricker snapped. In the aftermath of the near-death, his rage was as high as it had ever been, and now the inevitable shakes, as the Adrenalin began to subside, had set in. Which angered him further. 'I've got nothing for the press, Enright.'

Enright snapped back at him, 'You'd do well to be friendly.'

Bricker turned and pointed toward the towheaded youth, now groggily on his feet and being led away with his friend by the deputy. A folded newspaper stuck out of the erstwhile gunman's back pocket.

'See that?' Bricker demanded. 'If Billy had been two minutes later, that kid might have gone for his gun against me.'

'You were lucky,' Enright said.

'No. *They* were lucky. Because I could have gotten them both, Enright. The kid with the gun in hand first, and then Johnson. I would have had to hurry, so I would have had to shoot for the belly. If Billy hadn't come up, those two would be dead men right now.'

'They were drunk,' Enright blustered. 'They deserved—'

'Trust it to a newspaperman to talk about who deserves to die. Did you see that copy of your paper in his hip pocket? Do you suppose, maybe—just *maybe*—he was ready to fight me because he read your piece today, and figured I was over the hill? Do you suppose there's any chance at all that he almost died a minute ago because of what your stinking paper said about me today?'

'That's absurd,' Enright gasped.

'Maybe it is,' Bricker said. 'Maybe it isn't.'

'You're excited, you're—'

'You better *believe* I'm excited! I don't like killing, Enright. I don't like to kill people. Your rotten story might have helped him have the courage to try me out. If he had died, your paper would have killed him.'

The crowd was listening. Enright was pale. 'That's the silliest thing I ever heard!' he said weakly.

'You want a quote?' Bricker said. 'I'll give you a quote, Enright. Here it is. Stay out of my way. And stay off my back. Are you smart enough to understand *that*?'

Possibly Enright would have mustered an answer. But Bricker had already turned and strode away.

Chapter Two

The next afternoon, reminded by the note on the moose horns, **Bricker** went dutifully to the stage station to meet **John Wintle's** package. It was the hottest day of the year, so far over 100 that it didn't make any difference any more. Only a handful of people were on the street, dust devils hummed along, the sun beat down. Carrying a pound or two of evenly distributed dust over his sweaty carcass, Bricker was not in the best of moods. The fact that Billy Dean was hot-footing it right along with him was not helping matters.

The horizon to the east, out towards the badlands, was stained by the yellow dust of the oncoming stage. It was only minutes away, almost on time for once.

The stage appeared on the east road, rumbled closer, vanished behind buildings for a moment, reappeared at the far corner, creaking, groaning, thudding, grinding, rattling, shrilling with dust sifting off the horses and wheels.

The driver and shotgun man got down stiffly. They were typical, squat, middle-aged, roughly bearded and malodorous men.

'Howdy, Sheriff,' the driver said solemnly. 'Mayor.'

'Do you have some passengers, Andy?' the mayor asked.

'Sure do. Anybody seen that feller Wintle around?'

'I'm here for his delivery,' Bricker said. 'But go ahead and take care of your passengers first.'

The driver gave him an odd look, then limped to the stage proper. He swung the door open and peered inside. 'Here we are, come on out. We're in Hopewell.'

A beautiful young girl, wearing conservative Eastern dress, but with her long golden hair loose on her back, stepped daintily from the coach. She shaded her face far from the sun with a dainty hand, and looked around all sides. She was about seventeen, Bricker guessed.

On her heels came a boy a year or two younger, painfully skinny, with buck teeth, wearing a schoolish outfit complete with a flat-brimmed Quaker hat. He frowned at the girl. 'You see him, sis?'

'Not yet, Bobby,' she murmured.

Out of the stage came a bushy-haired boy of about ten, wearing short pants and ruffled shirt, and a little girl of about eight who was a chubby carbon copy of her older sister. Finally, appearing backside first as she clambered down backward from the high stage was a little one, a child who couldn't have been more than three, wearing ruffles and petticoats and a sucker stuck in her braids.

The five children, from the lovely girl to the near-baby, lined up along the front of the stage, frowning and shuffling. Each of them had a cardboard tag pinned to his coat on a string; the tags fluttered in the dusty wind.

The driver limped over to Bricker. 'Well, there y'are.'

'What?' Bricker said.

'I'm givin' you your delivery,' the driver said.

'When?' Bricker asked.

'They're *it*.'

'*Who?*' Bricker asked.

The driver gestured. 'Them.'

Bricker looked at the children. They looked at him. The smallest one sucked her thumb thoughtfully. The oldest girl looked puzzled and worried. The oldest boy looked blank. The younger boy grinned. The eight-year-old girl began to cry.

'Wait a minute,' Bricker told the driver. 'You're not trying to tell me—'

The driver looked puzzled. 'You come for Wintle's shipment?'

Bricker stared at the children. They stared at him. The hot wind pressed against their cheap, starchy, dark-coloured Eastern clothing. The name tags fluttered. Bricker couldn't believe it. It was some kind of mistake.

He walked over to the smaller boy, the ten-year-old, and looked at the tag tied to his coat button. It said, printed in pencil:

CLOVIS WINTLE
Deliver to: John Wintle,
Hopewell, N.M.

'Oh, no,' Bricker said. 'Oh, my God *no*.'

'Leggo of me!' Clovis yelped, and kicked him in the shin.

The sharp pain in his leg almost dropped Bricker to his knees. He hopped on one foot, fighting the impulse to slug the kid.

The mayor, who had been taking it all in, gasped, 'Sheriff, do I understand that *you* are to care for these waifs?'

'No,' Bricker groaned. 'It's a mistake.'

'No mistake,' the driver said cheerfully. 'You said you wanted Wintle's shipment. Well—*they're* Wintle's shipment, no doubt about it.'

'Sir?' the oldest girl said huskily. 'Are you here on behalf of our father?' She was strikingly beautiful, her hazel eyes troubled.

'I told him I'd get a package,' Bricker choked.

'I don't understand,' she said. 'Where is he?'

Billy Dean stepped forward, his hat clutched to his chest. 'Ma'am, let me introduce myself, I'm Billy Dean, deputy sheriff of this county, and this's Adam Bricker, my boss. Your dad asked the sheriff to meet you an' look after you until he could get back.'

'But where is he?' the girl demanded.

'Well, ma'am, he had a business trip he had to make—'

'Shut up,' Bricker growled. He turned to the girl. 'You're John Wintle's children?'

'Yes,' the girl murmured. 'I'm Adele, and this is Bobby, and Clovis, and Doreen, and the little one is Ellen. Doreen, hold Ellen's hand!'

Jarvis Fody put a heavy hand on Bricker's shoulder. 'Did you *know*—'

'Of course not,' Bricker said, trying to gather his wits. 'Miss uh—'

'Adele,' the beautiful girl smiled.

'Adele,' Bricker growled, 'your dad went to San Francisco. I don't know how soon he'll be back. You kids know anybody else in Hopewell?'

'No,' Adele said softly. 'No one.' She looked frightened.

The mayor hovered beside Bricker. 'Where you going to *keep* these children? How are you going to feed them? Have you got a chaperone? You can't keep that girl there in your house alone, she's a growd woman, practically. Did you know what Wintle was leaving you? How come you said you'd do this?'

'Because I'm a good old boy,' Bricker snarled. 'And no, I'm not going to take care of them. It's ridiculous. I thought Wintle had a box coming in or something. How could I take care of a bunch of kids like this?' He had a thought. 'Well, the city will have to care for them.'

The mayor gasped, 'The city has no facilities.'

'You'll have to find some!'

The mayor mopped his face. 'You understand we want no disputes, Sheriff. But I must point out that you assumed responsibility as an officer of the county. The county cannot ask the city to take over this situation. Proper division of government, et cetera. No, I'm afraid they're your responsibility, Sheriff, unless the board of county commissioners were to rule otherwise.'

'One county commissioner is in Tascosa,' Bricker groaned, 'another one is in Denver, and the third is dead.'

'Then it appears,' the mayor said, 'you're stuck.'

Bricker looked at the mayor. He looked at the clerk. He looked at the crowd and the crowd looked at him.

He turned to the kids, standing there in their dusty, shop-worn, cheap clothes, hot and tired and scared. Adele had picked up Ellen, the three-year-old, and held her, sleeping. Adele looked too frail for the task. Doreen was still crying, the tears making dusty rivulets down her face, and Clovis sucked his thumb defiantly, and Bobby, the older boy, frowned with the weight of responsibility beyond his years.

'We'll find someplace, Sheriff,' Bobby said manfully. 'I can work.'

Bricker sighed, making decisions. 'No, Bobby. That won't be necessary. You don't have to get a job just yet.'

He turned back to Adele, standing there with her sleeping burden. 'Your father is away on a trip, ma'am. But you can all stay at my place until he gets back. It isn't much—'

Billy Dean chirped. 'It's crummy, is what it is!'

Bricker gritted his teeth. '—but you're welcome there.'

'I don't want to be a bother,' Adele said nervously, but her radiant smile of relief began to burst through the worry.

'You won't be any bother at all,' Bricker smiled, thinking that when John Wintle got back, there was going to be a lesson in honesty.

'Thank you,' Adele breathed. 'Thank you *very* much. We'll try not to be a bother.' She was stunning.

'No bother at all.' Bricker lied.

Bobby held out a skinny hand. 'Thank you, Sheriff.'

Bricker smiled and shook the kid's hand, and, in an outburst of hopefulness, reached over to tousle Clovis's hair. Clovis kicked him in the shins again.

Chapter Three

Adam Bricker's house had never been of much concern to him, but as he trooped up to it with his covey of children, he wished it were a little more.

Stuck on the back of the rock and 'dobe jailhouse and office, the long frame structure, partly walled over with 'dobe mud, looked like a huge mudball likely to tumble down the slope into the dry creek ditch and vacant lot behind it. The whole thing leaned downhill, weeds choked the yard, birds' nests hung from shattered drain pipes, wasps buzzed in eaves, the porch was falling off. Being built onto the jail didn't help it any; the shade of the larger building made everything smell sort of musty and broken-down.

He had built most of the place himself, and had never claimed to be a carpenter or a draughtsman. The house consisted of four rooms, strung out one behind the other, and you went through one to get into the next. The biggest, the living room, was next to the jail, and the one Bricker had led the children into. Beyond was the kitchen, and beyond that the two bedrooms. The living room featured a rock fireplace that smoked, hand-me-down oak furniture and oil lamps, and dusty bare floor studded here and there with mouse droppings. The kitchen was walled with cabinets that had no doors, and against one wall was a work surface with a sink you could pump water up into. The stove was in good shape, and the big eating table was clean, although one leg was a little short. The bedrooms were stacked up with years' accumulation of junk; the first one, Bricker used as his own room, so it had a bed of ropes. The second bedroom was about hip-deep in junk.

Bricker pointed to an overstuffed chair in a corner. 'Guess you can put the little 'un down there for right now. I got some blankets.' He hustled to a closet and dragged out a quilt. Adele gently put Ellen down, and the child didn't even awaken as Bricker put the quilt around her.

From the back of the house came an ear-splitting crash.

'Bobby,' Adele ordered, 'go see what those two are into!'

'They can't hurt anything,' Bricker said dubiously.

Bobby looked grim. 'Don't bet on it. That's what the man who ran the train said in Kansas City.' He hustled out through the kitchen.

Adele winced. 'I'm sorry,' she murmured. 'We're already being an awful nuisance.'

'Now listen,' Bricker said gently. 'This isn't much of a place. They can't hurt it any. I'll just, uh. . . .' He looked around. 'I'll get a fire going. It's hot, but a fire ought to get the musty smell out. I got some food out there in the kitchen. We'll whomp up some biscuits or something, get some food in their guts. You can sleep in that back

27

bedroom, won't take but a minute for me to straighten it up a little. The other little ones can sleep next to you in the other bedroom. Bobby and I can batch it in here.'

'We can't put you out of your own room!'

'I sleep out here most of the time anyhow,' Bricker lied. 'So I can hear the jail next door,' he added.

'Well,' Adele murmured, looking around, 'we can manage, I'm sure, and when my father returns—' She caught her breath and began to sob, tears coursing down her cheeks. 'I'm sorry—I'm sorry—I'm being even a worse nuisance—'

Awkwardly Bricker took her into his arms and patted her. 'Now listen to me. You're as tired as any of them. That's all that's wrong. You just try not to worry about anything, hear?'

Adele, sweetly scented and womanlike, cuddled in his arms. Her face against his chest, she sniffled, 'Our mother died a year ago. We've been staying with my aunt, but she's poor, too, and I suppose my daddy didn't want us out here, but we had to come, Aunt Ellen wrote him and said we had to—'

'Of course your dad wants you,' Bricker grunted. 'Are you crazy? He's *wild* excited, he's so glad to have you out here!'

'Then why isn't he here?'

'He had business,' Bricker said. Once you started lying, you had to just keep going, he thought.

Adele managed a faint smile, and moved—accidentally—against him. 'You're a very nice man.' A hint of roguish fun appeared in her smile. 'I don't know how we'll ever repay you.' She moved again. Bump.

'Well,' Bricker said.

Adele's azure eyelids became veiled, and she smoothed a feline hand over his chest, as if idly—idly? —feeling the material of his vest. 'Having someone look after us . . . a big, brave, handsome man . . . it makes me all soft and squishy inside.' *Bump!*

'They broke the bed.'

Bricker turned. It was Bobby, back from the far reaches of the house.

'They what?' Bricker said.

'They broke your bed,' Bobby said morosely.

Doreen ran in from the kitchen. 'Adele, we're *hungry!*'

'Yeah!' Clovis whooped, coming up behind Doreen and trying to buckle her knees from behind.

'Stop that!' Doreen screamed, swinging at him.

Clovis backed off and jumped up and down, bow-legged, and thumbed his ears. 'Nyah, nyah, nyah!'

Doreen charged him. Clovis dodged. Doreen sprawled into the kitchen table and barked her leg and began to wail.

'I didn't do it!' Clovis cried. 'I didn't do it!'

'I *hate* you!' Doreen screamed, swinging at him from the floor.

'Take it easy,' Bricker said. 'Just calm down.'

'Missed me, missed me, nyah, nyah, nyah!' Clovis yelled gleefully, hopping around the kitchen.

Bricker strode into the kitchen, struggling with his temper. You had to be calm and fair and nice, he told himself. Everything he had ever read about fathering children said that. Calm and fair. Firm, maybe, but nice.

Bricker picked Clovis up by the back of the neck and swung him through the air.

'*Awrk!*' Clovis yelped.

Bricker swung him over his hip and crashed a good one, flat-handed, onto his backside. Before Clovis could react, Bricker's hand crashed down again. Dust flew from Clovis's pants. Bricker sat Clovis down, and the room had suddenly gotten dead silent.

'You want some, too?' Bricker asked Doreen, breathing hard.

'No!' Doreen mouthed, her eyes about as big around as pie plates.

'All right,' Bricker snapped. 'Clovis, you cause any more trouble, and now that I've got your butt dusted off, I'll give you a real licking. You savvy?'

Clovis, wide-eyed, with two tears on his cheeks, stared at him in mute shock.

'All right,' Bricker growled. 'Bobby, you take the luggage back in the back room. Shove all my stuff up against the wall. There are blankets back there. Make you some pallets on the floor. Unpack. Clovis, you go back there and fix the bed you just broke.'

Bricker glared at Doreen. 'You'll help me and your sister fix some grub. Right?'

'Right,' Doreen whispered, scared out of her wits.

'All right,' Bricker grunted.

Bricker got the water pumped up. Doreen by this time had a fire started with too much kindling. Bricker said nothing about the mistake.

At the table, Adele had her sleeves rolled up on pretty arms, and was peeling potatoes. She had gotten out some greens and dried beef, too. Bricker nodded encouragement and went to the cabinet to get out flour.

'What are you going to do?' she asked as he carried the flour can to the table.

'Oh, I thought I'd make some biscuits.'

'Listen,' she said, excited. 'Maybe we could make some dumplings, too.'

Bricker stared at her. 'Dumplings?'

'You've got some apples underneath the sink. I could core them for you and we could make dumplings.'

'I dunno,' Bricker muttered. 'Biscuits is one thing. Dumplings are something else.'

'The children would love them.'

'I dunno,' Bricker repeated. Hell, he didn't want to make dumplings. Biscuits were something a man baked to eat with gravy, so they would stick to his ribs. Biscuits were survival. Dumplings seemed sort of feminine and wasteful and stupid.

'Please?' Adele begged.

'Well,' Bricker growled, 'I won't core any apples.'

'I'll do that. And I'll make the brown sugar sauce and everything. If you just make the dough, I'll do all the rest. The children will just love them!'

'Well, all right.'

'Oh, thank you!' Adele beamed.

'I'm not going to any extra pains, though.'

'You're such a nice man. I know you have all your duties with the city, keeping the law and everything.'

'Don't believe everything you hear,' Bricker grunted, sifting flour. 'Hopewell's not as wild as people let on. We've got gangs out in the hills, and our share of

31

rowdies here in town. But it's no wild West show every night.'

'I don't imagine it would dare be,' Adele murmured, 'with you here.'

Bricker grinned, then snuffed the grin because it came from feeling puffed up. 'Besides. I've got Billy Dean. Like right now, he's watching after everything for me.'

'Is Billy Dean the tall boy who was with you when we got here?'

'That's the one.'

'He seemed very nice.'

'Well,' Bricker said, 'he does a pretty good job. He only sticks himself in the chest with his badge about once a week, and he finds the way to the office by himself almost every day.'

'I think you're putting me on,' Adele smiled.

Bricker said nothing, intent on his dough.

He was not at all sure what would happen later. He intended to get a wire or two off to San Francisco yet tonight, to start looking for John Wintle. And he couldn't let Billy Dean walk all the rounds alone. Then there was the business of trying to determine just who had to maintain custody of this bunch of kids until Wintle could be dragged back. Not to mention continuing the search for the gangs out in the badlands, and the problem of Enright sniping at him in the paper just a couple months ahead of the election.

In a little while, Bobby came back from the bedroom with the news that Clovis had fallen asleep in the corner. Bricker put Bobby to work setting the table. Adele had the apples and everything ready for the dumplings, but was having trouble getting the dough cut into squares and folded around the fruit.

'I'll do that,' Bricker grunted. 'Help your brother.'

As he shouldered her aside, someone rapped on the door in the living room.

'Tell him to wait,' Bricker said, his back turned.

'I'm already in,' a voice said.

Bricker glanced over his shoulder. Harold Enright stood in the door between rooms.

'You got good manners,' Bricker muttered.

'What are you *doing*?' Enright asked, incredulous.

'Baking apple dumplings.'

'Apple dumplings!'

'That's what I said, Enright. Are you deaf? What's on your mind? Are you looking for trouble? I got all these kids in here asleep, so keep your voice down. They need food so I'm cooking 'em apple dumplings. Is your paper against apple dumplings?'

Enright began to grin. 'I came over here to get the story on the children. But this beats anything I ever saw.'

Adele, wide-eyed, said softly. 'You want to interview *us*?'

Enright seemed to notice her for the first time. 'You're the oldest?'

'Yes.'

Bricker dried his hands on a towel. 'Adele, finish these up. Do them the way I started, see? Enright, I want a word with you in the other room.'

Adele obeyed, and Bricker took the newspaperman into the living room.

'Listen,' Bricker grated. 'About Wintle. These kids think he's a big man around here, Enright.'

'They *what*?'

'Just go along with them,' Bricker said. 'Don't say anything that might let 'em know he's been a drunk. If they act like he's a big man, just agree with 'em. And when you write a story up on them, make sure you don't say anything about their daddy that they'd read and figure out the truth from.'

'I don't know,' Enright muttered. 'A newspaper ought to serve the truth.'

'You better do what I say.'

'Are you threatening me?' Enright flared.

'You're goddam right I am!'

In the chair, little Ellen stirred and began to cry.

'Now see what you went and did?' Bricker said. 'You do what I tell you, Enright, or I'll find something in your shop that's illegal if I have to tear it apart piece by piece.'

'You wouldn't,' Enright said.

Bricker looked at him.

'You would,' Enright said.

Bricker went over and picked Ellen up, awkwardly. 'It's okay, hon,' he said, feeling clumsy.

'I never thought I'd see it,' Enright breathed, watching in awe. 'A sheriff in this town. Making dumplings. Taking care of foundlings. Threatening a newspaper editor. Why, Bricker? Let me ask you that: *Why?*'

'Because,' Bricker glowered, 'I'm a sweet person.'

Chapter Four

First thing the next morning Bricker trudged around the jailhouse and went inside and checked the prisoners. The jail smelled sour of vomit, and of course some of the prisoners said they were dying. Bricker relocked the front door and walked downtown. The dirt streets lay almost vacant, and the wind hadn't gotten up yet to swirl the deep yellow dust. The sun beat down with thin, intense heat. It was just a little after 6 a.m.

To an outsider, he thought, it would have looked like a very nice, very quiet, very peaceful little town. He wondered where the gangs were outside the municipal limits, and how he might trick them into capture. The last time he had called for volunteers for a posse, he had gotten two twelve-year-olds and a senile schoolteacher. Now the Wintle kids had compounded his problems. He couldn't keep them. He planned to make every effort to find Wintle, but there were no guarantees. What if Wintle never came back? What happened to the kids? They were foundlings. There would be just about as many volunteers to take over five kids as there had been for his last posse.

With the exception of offers to care for Adele, he thought.

Depressed, he walked to Bagwell's Saloon. The front door stood open. He went inside. It was dark and smelled dusty and brewery-like of beer. All the chairs were upside down on the tables and there were no customers. U. S. Bagwell stood halfway back in the big room, attacking the floor with a broom. A woman, Mrs Bagwell, was behind the bar, fiddling with a coffeepot suspended over the small fireplace.

'Come in this house!' Bagwell yelled, spying him. Bagwell was a big man, enormously fat, with a wooden peg where his left hand was supposed to be. 'You sonofagun, what brings you out this early?'

Bricker walked to the bar and leaned on it. 'Kids get up early.'

Mrs Bagwell, a small, mild-eyed woman who had once been very beautiful, smiled and shook her head. 'We heard about that. If we hadn't been so busy last night, we would have come over to see how you were doing.'

'I'm doing all right,' he lied.

'Anything we can do,' Mrs Bagwell said.

'You could offer me some of that coffee.'

'You poor thing, of course! Honey, pull up a chair for the sheriff. Now, Adam Bricker, you set yourself right down there and I'll give you some coffee, and I have some hot rolls in the kitchen.' She bustled out.

Bagwell sat down with Bricker and leaned forward expectantly. 'You figure on keeping care of those kids quite a while?'

'I don't know,' Bricker admitted.

'You figure John Wintle is coming back?'

'He's coming back.'

'When?'

'I don't know. But he's coming back.'

Bagwell rubbed his cheek with his wooden stump. 'Mighty hard to find a man like John Wintle in a place like San Francisco, if he doesn't want to be found.'

'He's coming back,' Bricker repeated.

The day dragged. Bricker sent wires to general delivery in San Francisco, to the police department there, and to the sheriff's office. He also queried Wells Fargo and ascertained that Wintle had been listed as an arriving passenger in Santa Fe, and the train company said he had bought a ticket for the coast. Bricker told himself it would be possible to locate Wintle quickly.

It was hard to understand men like Wintle. Bricker had wanted kids. It hadn't happened, and then his wife had died so suddenly. Why did people like Wintle abandon them? Thinking about it, Bricker felt deep anger building in his belly.

Riding down a side street to get to the jail, he noticed an odd atmosphere right away. There was more activity on the streets than normal for late afternoon, but it was purposeless. Men stood around in small groups, talking, with newspapers under their arms. Some of them glanced at him, and the grins flashed and then were quickly extinguished.

Puzzled, Bricker reached the jail. His copy of the *Record* was on the porch. Picking it up on the way inside, he checked the office. Billy Dean wasn't there, but he found a note saying his deputy had gone shopping with Adele and would be back soon. The note said Mrs Bagwell was back in the house, watching after the little ones.

Collapsing into his swivel chair, he opened the day's paper.

His insides dropped.

He read:

THE APPLE DUMPLING GANG

Hopewell, already known far and wide as the friendly haven for the Hash Knife Outfit, the Hole in the Wall Gang, and the Stillwell Mob, not to mention various other assorted and sundry criminals, is paying host to another band today.

The group is known as The Apple Dumpling Gang.

The Wintle children, who arrived here yesterday (see story, this page) are staying with Sheriff Adam Bricker. This editor paid a visit last night and found the sheriff up to his elbows in pie dough and flour. Our defender of law and order was making apple dumplings for his new charges.

It was a touching scene. Hopewell can be proud that its sheriff is a good cook and makes apple dumplings. Surrounded by his Apple Dumpling Gang, the ageing sheriff seemed happy and content.

While the Apple Dumpling Gang was cavorting in the pie dough at the sheriff's house, it is reported on good authority that the Stillwell Mob tried to hold up the midnight special from Santa Fe to Albuquerque. They were beaten off by special train guards, and pursued in the direction of our fair city. As usual they escaped. No word was heard from the Hash Knife

Outfit or the Hole in the Wall Gang, but you can be sure they also were busy.

Also, while the sheriff and his Apple Dumpling Gang treated their tasters to syrup and brown sugar, a local store was broken into (see story, this page). The sheriff was not available for comment. Washing pots and pans, Sheriff?

An election is scheduled for our county this fall, and it will be interesting to see whether voters want a lawman who will enforce the law or bake apple dumplings while crime runs rampant in our streets. We all applaud humanitarian activities by any person. But let's have first things first! A sheriff's job is *not* apple dumplings.

Bricker wadded the paper and hurled it against the far wall.

Back in the cellblock, one of the prisoners saw it.

'Hey, Sheriff,' he called. 'If you're through with that paper, can we see it?'

If the bucket that sailed through the door and crashed into the bars had had just a little greater velocity, it might have gone right through.

Late in the afternoon, in a box canyon about a dozen miles west of Hopewell, Preacher Addison looked up from his copy of the paper at the men surrounding him in the partially burned-out house. It was hot and dusty, even in the hidden canyon despite trees and a little creek nearby, and the tarp across the burned-out end of the log cabin let in too much sunlight and sifting dust. Despite these inconveniences, two of Addison's men were stretched out on the floor, snoozing lightly.

Another was piled up against the wall in a sitting position, his sombrero pulled down over his eyes. Only Tommy Delbert, the oldest of Addison's Hole in the Wall Gang, at age nineteen, was reasonably alert.

'This,' Preacher Addison said, rattling the newspaper on the rickety tabletop, 'is real interesting.' A tall, gaunt man with lung trouble, Addison at twenty-four had profoundly more experience than any present gang members.

Jeff Simms, on the floor, opened one eye. 'What is, boss?'

Addison tapped the paper with a fingernail. 'Seems like our law friend in Hopewell has a problem.'

Donnie Hawkins lifted his sombrero. 'You thinking about pulling a job *in* Hopewell?'

'Maybe,' Addison said.

Jeff Simms sat up. 'What kind of a job?'

'Maybe,' Addison said, 'the bank.'

The effect was miraculous. Simms and Hawkins got wide awake. Delbert forgot to polish his revolver. Fred Green blinked and paid attention.

'You think Bricker would be *that* busy?' Green asked.

'It says here in the paper, he's baking apple dumplings for them and every other goddam thing.'

Green frowned. 'Lemme see.'

Addison handed the paper over, and while Green scowled at the job of deciphering the words, he went on. 'We've talked about that bank before. We've always let it go because of Bricker. But now the paper is down on him and he's got these kids, and maybe he's thinking nobody is *ever* going to hit it. So maybe we ought to hit it.'

'How long,' Simms asked, 'are them kids likely to be in town?'

'It doesn't say. I think we ought to move fast, if we want to do it.'

'Well,' Hawkins said, 'I don't like it.'

'I like it,' Delvert snapped, eager to argue with anybody.

Green looked dubious, but said, 'I'm willing to give 'er a try.'

Addison looked at Simms.

'Hell,' Simms grinned. 'Why not?'

'Okay,' Addison said, feeling relief mixed with a new kind of tension. 'It's decided, then. We'll hit the Hopewell Bank—*if* we can work out a good plan fast enough to take advantage of these kids being there, and all.'

Hawkins brought the pencil and sheets of paper. Addison began to draw the street plan of Hopewell. His men gathered around, watching intently, as he explained.

Addison felt himself picking up a steam-head of confidence. He had wanted to go in, head-to-head with Adam Bricker, for a long time. He was glad they were finally going to do it. He felt confident, too, in his gang. They hadn't worked as a unit for a very long time, and the boys were all young. But they were good, and, with the exception of Delbert's trigger-happy moods, controllable and efficient. They had been blooded. This would be the biggest job in the history of the gang, either with this membership or earlier ones. It was going to be memorable. He was looking forward to it—

Saturday, at 2 p.m.

Chapter Five

'You could sue him.'

Adam Bricker looked morosely across the café table at his friend Jarvis Fody. 'Why do that? It would just give him more publicity—make it look like he got my goat.'

Mayor Oliver Steed, the third person at the table in an isolated corner of the café, nodded thoughtfully. 'Quite so,' he said. 'If you sue Enright, you only add fuel to the fire.'

'What about the fire that's already lit?' Fody asked angrily.

'So a few people are laughing at me,' Bricker grunted.

'It's not just that, Adam. Don't you see how this editorial is an open invitation to every rumdum crook in the country to come into Hopewell and try his hand?'

'That's true,' the mayor nodded. 'I hadn't thought of that.'

'That's ridiculous,' Bricker argued. 'Who's going to believe what he reads in the papers?'

Fody shook his head slowly. 'Adam, you're one of the

stubbornest, orneriest people I ever met. Look: suppose you're a criminal, you're hiding out somewhere around here, you read in the paper that the sheriff is baby-sitting a batch of snot-nose kids; you're going to say, "Hey! Let's go in and rob the Wells Fargo office while he's so busy!"'

'Or,' the mayor added, nervous, 'the bank.'

'Right,' Fody snapped.

'Oh, dear,' the mayor murmured.

'Nobody's going to rob the bank,' Bricker snapped.

'It's possible,' Fody insisted. 'Listen. It could happen.'

'If they try to rob the bank, I'll stop them, that's all.'

'You could sue Enright. Get an injunction against him printing anything more—*anything* more—about how busy you are, or where you're at. The judge would go along with it. He'll be here in a couple of days. You could shut Enright's water off for him.'

'And,' the mayor observed meekly. 'It might have additional benefits.'

Bricker looked at the two of them. Finally he said, 'You mean it might help me get re-elected.'

'If that's a side effect, Adam, be thankful for it.'

'No,' Bricker said. 'I don't fight that way.'

'Listen,' Fody said, more impatient than ever. 'When we capitalized this bank here, we put in three thousand dollars apiece, eight of us. Right now, even with things tough, there's about fourteen thousand in gold lying over there in the vault. That's plenty enough to get some gangsters to come in here and try to break it if they have the *slightest* encouragement—which is just what Enright is giving them.'

'Nobody is going to get away with robbing the bank,' Bricker said.

The Friday morning sun blasted the dirt streets of Hopewell.

Bricker walked down towards the bank, more to reassure himself about its impregnability than anything.

He was tired. He had felt the apple dumpling editorial yesterday with more than the usual anger and dismay. After reading it, his impulse had been to stay in the office and pretend to be busy, but he had realized angrily that this would be interpreted with even more glee. He had forced himself to circulate as usual.

Most of the ribbing had been good-natured enough. Criswell the barber asked if he could also bake cookies, because there was a church supper coming up. Young, who ran the livery, said his old lady wanted to borrow the dumpling recipe, and how did he keep the tops from getting too hard. Herb Stein, the café owner, said he needed another cook.

It hadn't made him in a very good mood last night. He had walked his beat and, thank God, it had been unusually quiet. He had been able to leave it with Billy Dean about midnight, and head home.

There he had found Adele with two suitors—two of the very punks Bricker detested—sitting out in the side yard in the pitch black, for corn sakes, holding hands or something, tittering like idiots. And inside the house, Bobby was mopping the floor where Ellen had slipped again, and Clovis was taunting Doreen, and Doreen was trying to hit him with walnuts she was chucking all over the house from a sack that had been neatly put in a cupboard. And at this point, Bricker—tired and disgusted and pushed a little too far—had bellowed into the yard for Adele to get her blankety-blank tail in here, and for you two punks to get out of here and don't come back or you'll be on the other side of this wall in the jail, yes, you read me right, sonny, in jail, and for Clovis to stop picking on Doreen, and for Doreen to stop chucking the Go—the gosh-darned nuts, and for Bobby to stop mopping the stupid floor and put a stupid diaper on that kid if she can't control herself.

At which point Adele fled to the back bedroom, the suitors vanished, Bobby stared in mute shock, Clovis dived into bed, Doreen ran for the closet, and Ellen wet herself on the puma rug in front of the fireplace.

And Bricker, left suddenly in a house quiet with shock and fear, felt guilty as hell. Which depressed him even worse.

But that, he reminded himself now, had been yesterday.

Today he would be hearing from his wires to San Francisco.

Standing now at the bank corner, with the last sounds of the morning chimes still echoing, Bricker looked the bank over, seeking reassurance.

There it stood, a two-story building, brick and stone, solid, permanent, strong, solvent. Stonework curlicues decorated the high eaves and windows, but there was no nonsense about the walls, a foot thick, and the fact that there were only two doors, one on the corner and one around back into the alley with a steel security door inside the regular one. No nonsense about the big vault inside, either, Bricker thought.

It wouldn't be an easy bank to rob, he reflected. Because the back doors were closed and locked always, except when armed guards stood by as Wells Fargo money came in that way, any robbers would have to come right in the front. The corner was broad, and the stores on the other side of the street would offer the law perfect gun positions. The street ran straight for a couple of blocks in either direction along Main, and the side street was wide enough and straight enough, too, to mean that horsemen trying to make a get-away would be under continuous fire for a fatal amount of time.

'Do you always stand on corners looking at bank buildings?'

The voice, soft, feminine, and tinged with friendly irony, made him turn. The woman smiling up at him from beneath the edge of her dark blue parasol was in her thirties, wearing a long blue summer dress with hoops and ruffles of an understated, no-nonsense variety. Her face was slender, lighted by a pair of quick brown eyes and a piquant mouth that was, right now, at its best because of the smile. Helen Jefferson owned the Bright Light Dance Hall, but although she was beautiful, she didn't much look the part. She looked more like someone's wife . . . which Bricker had occasionally thought about with some seriousness.

'Do I always look at banks?' Bricker repeated. 'Huh-uh. Not when there's a pretty woman to look at.'

'You're positively courtly,' Helen said, 'and at eight o'clock in the morning, too.'

'Well,' Bricker growled, 'that's all I got to do, you know. Sit around and think up nice things to say to the ladies. And bake apple dumplings.'

Helen winced. 'I saw that. You hadn't told me about the children.'

'Well I figured if I did, you'd be right over there, fiddling around wanting to help.'

She looked at him thoughtfully. 'Would that be so bad? Having me around?'

'You got enough to do,' Bricker said. His effort to hide his true feelings made his voice gruff. 'You got a business to run.'

'You make such a fetish of being independent,' she said.

'Is that bad?' he asked, stung.

'It might be . . . when people truly want to help.'

'Well, I'm edgy. I didn't mean anything, Helen. You know that.'

'I know,' she said softly.

They looked at each other for a moment, and he thought how beautiful she was. She was a widow. She was a good woman, too, he thought. If he wasn't just a beat-up lawman getting old . . . if his first wife's death hadn't hurt so badly, and for such a long time. . . .

She asked, 'Would you be angry if I came by to try to help?'

'If you came by to help, yeah, I'd be mad.'

'Oh.'

'If you just came by,' he added dubiously, 'that'd be different.'

She smiled broadly. 'I'll remember the distinction.'

Bricker jammed his hands in his pockets. 'I got to git.'

'Jail business?'

'Well, I got to check on the prisoners.'

She nodded. 'Expect me to come by.'

'I'll count on it.'

They looked at each other again.

'Well,' Helen said, almost faltering.

Bricker walked away.

On the way to the jail, he thought about the way things might be if he had a better job, or even a more secure one. He told himself he was being dumb and sentimental.

At the jail, Bobby Wintle had everything piled up on one corner of Bricker's desk, and was washing it. Bricker stood uncomfortably just inside the door because the whole floor gleamed wetly. The whole place smelled of soap and water, the guns had been oiled on the rack, the broken door into the cellblock had been patched with a piece of cardboard, and even the moose had been dusted. The place smelled different, too. Like clean.

'What are you doing at my desk?' Bricker asked gruffly.

Bobby smiled. 'Just straightening it up for you.'

'There's a lot of important stuff on that desk. It's all arranged.'

'I know,' Bobby replied quickly. 'I'm keeping everything in order.'

Bricker relaxed. 'Well, you're doing a good job,' he said.

'What do you want me to do after this?'

'Nothing. Take it easy. You've worked hard already this morning.'

'I'd like to do more,' Bobby said.

Bricker turned to him. 'Why?'

Bobby frowned. 'The little kids don't . . . understand. But Adele and me, we had a talk.' He paused, and then the words came in a rush. 'We know our dad might have skipped out.'

'Balderdash,' Bricker grunted.

'We know,' Bobby said firmly. 'And if he *has* skipped out, and ain't coming back—'

The door swung open behind Bricker. He turned to see Herb Stein, the blacksmith. Stein was huge, brawny, and covered with soot as usual. His bald head glowed like a signal lantern under the black.

'You know who just go off the train?' Stein demanded.

'Billy the Kid,' Bricker guessed.

'The colonel,' Stein said.

'Oh, God,' Bricker said.

Bobby asked, 'Who's the colonel?'

'His name is Clydesdale,' Bricker explained wearily. 'T. T. Clydesdale. He used to live here. He lives in Kansas City or someplace back East like that now. He was one of the men who helped capitalize the bank. He comes here once or twice a year, and he always causes a riot. The last time, he was pretty quiet. When he left, the preacher's wife ran off with him. You remember that, Herb?'

Stein's grin winked through. 'I remember. She was some little—'

'Where is he now?' Bricker cut in.

'Well, he headed for Bagwell's Saloon.'

'It figures,' Bricker muttered, hitching up his gunbelt a notch. 'I better get over there.'

Bobby said, 'I sure would like to do more work—anything I can do to help.'

'I can't think of anything,' Bricker snapped.

'I could go through all these wanted posters,' Bobby suggested earnestly.

'What for?'

'Well, sir, I could get out the ones of guys that've been caught, and then I could arrange the others, and study 'em.'

'Study them for *what*?'

'If somebody came to town, and they were wanted, maybe I could help you spot them.'

Bricker almost exploded at the idiocy of it. He restrained himself. The kid was serious, and he wanted to help. Which was more than most people around here wanted to do.

'That's a real good idea,' he said softly. 'You do that, Bobby.'

Bobby's face lit up. 'I'll get right on it, as soon as I set the mousetraps.'

Bricker started for the door.

He hurried for the saloon. Of all the times for the colonel to come around on one of his semi-occasional hell-raising expeditions, this had to be the worst possible, Bricker thought.

Bagwell's was just ahead, and a couple of local storekeepers larruped onto the porch and ducked gleefully inside as Bricker approached. They weren't running from him; they were going to see the colonel. As Bricker

stepped up onto the porch, a ragged cheer burst forth
from inside, and as Bricker went through the swinging
doors, he caught the colonel's drawling, nasal voice in-
toning one of his speeches.

About a dozen men had already gathered, standing
around among the chair-heaped tables. They were
grinning and giggling and nudging each other. Up on
the bar stood a short, fat, pinkly gleaming man in a
yellow suit and vest, brown derby hat, white spats and
black high top shoes. A stickpin glittered on his tie, and
he was wearing about six rings on his pudgy fingers. He
swirled a cane with one hand, a straight, ebony-
handled walking stick, and balanced a mug of beer in
the other.

Bricker stood against the wall, feeling slightly ill, as
the colonel jumped nimbly down off the bar and
came through the crowd toward him. The others
immediately began talking loudly among themselves,
yelling, in fact, out of excitement over the visit and the
pleasure of getting free beer at nine in the morning.

'Ah, Sheriff,' the colonel intoned, tapping Bricker
on the chest with the head of his cane. 'It is a distinct
pleasure, my good man, to see you once more.'

'Are you here for a bank audit?' Bricker said, gritting
his teeth.

'Of course. A routine matter, I assure you.'

'I think you're lying.'

The colonel drew himself up to his full height of five
feet, four. 'You besmirch my integrity, sir! If it were
later in the day, or if I were not in serious need of a visit
to facilities, I should be forced to challenge you to a
duel.'

'Why are you really here?' Bricker pressed.

'The bank audit is legitimate, sir, I assure you,' the colonel said. He glanced around and lowered his voice. 'Also, and in strictest confidence, there was a slight marital mixup in a suburb of Kansas City, yes . . . a local attorney of some repute, his charming wife Betsy, and myself. . . . You see, sir, Betsy sought the solace of an older and more sympathetic gentleman, a true noble among men, and, being the samaritan I am, I sought to succour her in her distress. Her husband—'

'You're out of Kansas City until he cools off,' Bricker said.

'You might put it that way, yes.'

'All right,' Bricker growled. 'We've got a lot of trouble around here right now, a lot of tension. Keep your nose clean this time, Colonel, or so help me, I'll throw you in that jail until the walls fall down from natural erosion.'

'Sir,' the colonel said, 'again you affront me. I plan only to conduct my business, assisted by my apt and diligent bookkeeper, and to, perhaps, quaff a few fragrant goblets of relaxing vintage brew.'

'You brought a bookkeeper?' Bricker asked.

'Yes, a charming girl, her name is Delores, and while she is very young, she exhibits extremely facile mental capacity, not to mention great digital dexterity. She is at the hotel at present, I believe, resting mind and body for the strenuous hours of mathematical calculations which lay ahead.'

'Check the books,' Bricker warned, 'and keep Delores company. But stay out of trouble. I don't have time to mess with you.'

'I plan,' the colonel said, 'no other activity. This afternoon, of course, I may imbibe to a moderate degree, but you may be sure, my good man, that civic disturbance is the farthest item from my mind. I shall cause you not a scintilla of concern, not a scintilla.'

'All right,' Bricker said, turning toward the door.

'I worry about you, noble sir,' the colonel called after him. 'You take life far too seriously.'

Bricker went outside.

Maybe, he thought, the colonel would behave.

Behind him came the colonel's voice inside the saloon. 'Noble old friends and new acquaintances, let me make a suggestion. Let us quaff the contents of this majestic keg to the dregs. I intend, in a word, to get drunk together.'

Chapter Six

Well outside town, beyond Tightwad Hill, the Stillwell Mob discussed strategy. The four men sat cross-legged under the trees, smoking. Even a casual onlooker would have noticed that they were an older, and perhaps cannier, band than the Hole in the Wall Gang. Fred Stillwell was thirty-two, a black-bearded man with broad shoulders and huge, powerful forearms. Even older was the one known as Jersey Jack, a bald, muscular, hulking man with a smashed face. Dan Harp, rolling a fresh cigarette now with slender, pale hands, had the cold air of a professional gunman about him, and was no kid at twenty-eight. Only Marshall, the newest member, blond-headed and with brilliant blue-green eyes, could claim real youth; he was twenty-two.

'We'll do it, then,' Stillwell said, scratching his beard.

'When?' Marshall asked quietly.

'What's wrong with now?' Dan Harp asked.

'No, no,' Stillwell snapped. 'We got to look things over first. Somebody has to go in, make sure they don't have any special guards, plan the best escape route through the streets, get a look at the vault, if he can, so we'll know how much dynamite to haul in there for it.'

'I carry duh hynamite, huh, boss?' Jersey Jack grunted, rocking on his buttocks.

'You'll go to town,' Stillwell told Marshall.

'Why me?' Marshall asked, not in protest.

'We know they've got no posters up on you, you being new.'

Marshall nodded cheerfully. 'All right. I'll go then.'

'We have to plan careful,' Stillwell pointed out. 'The kids will keep Bricker busy, I guess, like the paper says they are. But we don't want any chances we don't have to take. It's still risky, and if we weren't broke as hell, I'd have never suggested it.'

'What should I look for?' Marshall asked.

'What I said. What's the best street to go in? Where will we leave the horses? How much crossfire do we have to worry about after the explosion? How many people likely inside the bank on a Saturday? Where's the vault? How big? Are there shades at the windows? What about guards? We know it's two blocks from the jail to the bank corner, and we know we could ride right down Main Street, but what are the alternatives if Bricker gets the word fast and manages to deputize some people?'

Marshall frowned, digesting the questions. 'It does sound tough, all right.'

'Pull this job,' Stillwell said, repeating himself, 'and we can split up, head south of the border, lay low for a long, long time. Without this job, we're stuck here for more penny-ante train jobs, and I don't want to mess with any more of those special train guards.'

'We do it tomorrow, then?' Dan Harp asked.

'Unless Marshall spots a problem. Yes.'

'In the morning?'

Stillwell thought about it. 'I think we'd be better off to do it as late as possible. In the morning there are farmers with wagons all over the street, and for all we know there could be lots of people in the bank. No, the later in the day, the better.'

'Noon, then,' Harp said. 'The bank closes at noon.'

'The bank in Hopewell stays open until two,' Stillwell said.

'Two, then,' Harp said.

'Two,' Stillwell agreed. 'Any questions?'

No one spoke.

'Git,' Stillwell told Marshall. 'But be careful. Take the hay wagon, wear your sodbuster pants, so you'll look like a farmer. Nobody ever pays attention to farmers.'

Marshall got to his feet. 'Right. I'll be careful. I ought to be back by nightfall.'

There was no doubt, Bricker thought, that the colonel would cause him some trouble. The most hopeful line was to believe that it might be relatively minor trouble, like an outbreak of the smallpox or a tornado. It would be a good idea to let his deputy, Billy Dean, know about the impending disaster as soon as possible.

Crossing the bank corner, Bricker glanced toward the building again and saw a rotund, bearded figure in the doorway. The man wore a dark suit with sausage legs and arms, and a velvet vest. As manager of the Hopewell bank Tim Whitaker had reason to look worried, and he did. He waved at Bricker, inviting him to come over.

Bricker walked to the bank doorway. 'Have you heard the news, Tim?'

Whitaker, about fifty, was looking older this morning. 'I heard,' he said, transferring his cigar from one side of his bearded mouth to the other. 'Step inside a minute, will you, Adam?'

Bricker complied. Inside the high, echoing lobby of the bank, dust motes hung in the shaft of sunlight entering the front windows. 'He wants a study of the books,' he told Bricker.

'It's his privilege,' Bricker said.

'By the time he leaves town, the bank will have lost a dozen customers. They come in and say, "I never knew *a drunk* was a stockholder in this bank, give me my dad-blasted money and I'll bury it in the yard."'

Bricker turned to go. 'He really might stay sober, you know.'

'The sun,' Whitaker said, 'may rise in the west, too.'

Bricker left, and went back to his office. Inside he found Bobby Wintle and Billy Dean. Both of them were poring over WANTED posters.

'Howdy, boss!' Dean grinned.

'What are you doing?' Bricker asked.

'Checking these posters. We might have any number of wanted guys in town—you know?'

Bricker took a deep breath. 'Billy, will you step outside a minute, please?'

Dean winked at Bobby Wintle and ducked onto the porch.

'Look, Billy,' Bricker said as gently as he could, 'you

can look over at posters all you want. You always could. Why the sudden rush right now?'

Dean frowned manfully. 'There might be somebody in town.'

'That was true yesterday. Why the interest *right now*?'

'Well,' Dean said slowly, his head down, 'maybe if a man catches a criminal, even if he's just a deputy, I mean—I mean, well, if I was to do something good like that, maybe folks would set up and take notice. Some.'

Bricker didn't get it. 'You feeling left out of something?'

'Shucks no! Not that. But—well—' Dean got pink around the ears. 'Well—see—look: I know Adele likes you. I mean she likes you *a lot*. But if I was to do something pretty good, maybe she'd notice *me*.'

The light dawned. 'You want to impress Adele, eh?'

Dean got redder. 'I know she likes you best, boss, but it don't look like you care much for her. That's understandable. You're so old.'

'Yeah,' Bricker grunted. 'Me being so ancient.'

'I didn't mean *that*! I—'

Bricker put his hand on his deputy's shoulder. 'Billy, you want Adele, you figure you can impress her, that's great. You're right. I'm about three hundred years too old for her.'

'I didn't mean to—'

'I don't want her,' Bricker said candidly. 'She's pretty and cute and a lovely girl. But don't worry about trying to beat my time. This is one race I'm not entering.'

'That's great,' Dean grinned. 'Now if I could just get her attention—'

'You'll figure a way,' Bricker said. 'But right now the colonel is over at Bagwell's. Get over there and keep your eye on things.'

'Yes, sir,' Dean said, relieved. 'I'll get right on it!' He started away, then remembered something. 'Oh! I left some stuff from the telegraph office on your desk.'

Bricker went back inside. Bobby was still working over the posters. Bricker leaned a straight chair against the wall and read the wires. The West Coast law-enforcement agencies were very polite about acknowledging messages. None had seen John Wintle.

'News?' Bobby asked hopefully.

He was a nice kid. 'Too early for news,' Bricker lied. Bobby didn't hide his disappointment well. 'I see.'

'How's the work coming?'

Bricker asked to change the subject.

'Great.' Bobby brightened. 'I think I'm learning a lot. I plan to go out pretty soon and look around.'

'Well, it can't hurt anything. But just don't bother anybody. Right?'

'What if I spot a criminal?' Bobby asked.

'Well,' Bricker grunted, 'you just walk up behind him and stick your finger in his back and say, "Hands up!" Then you get somebody to come find me on the double.'

'Will a finger work?' Bobby asked seriously.

'A finger works fine,' Bricker said. 'I knew a man once—' He stopped. Bobby was not old enough for that story. 'I got to get moving. Remember what I said.'

'Yes, sir!' Bobby called after him.

Standing out in front of the jail, Bricker thought

about his next step. The telegrams were a keen disappointment. If he had been running true to form, Wintle would have gotten arrested by now on a public drunk charge. What was going on? Bricker had heard of cases where men simply dropped from view, were never seen or heard from again. Was Wintle going to be one of those? If so, what was going to happen to these kids?

Distantly, he heard a sound like someone chopping green wood. He heard grunting, too, and scuffling feet. Someone was busy, he thought.

More sounds, a sharp yelp, a male voice, in pain . . .

Suddenly Bricker recognized the noises and cursed himself for daydreaming. He turned and jarred off the porch, running around the jail towards his own back yard.

The scene was exactly what he had finally figured out. The only variables were the number of participants and the audience.

Instead of only two men fighting, there were four, all young, and all swinging their fists, feet and anything else handy in a tightly knotted, swirling, dusty ball in the side yard beside his house. It was one hell of a free-for-all, the Italian boy who worked at the store, a couple of drovers whom Bricker didn't recognize, and a blond kid from the post office. Maybe at one time the two drovers had been trying to stay together in the thing, but it had gone beyond that now. One of them was on the ground, his clothes half torn off and his face bloody, and the Italian was trying carefully to stomp his face in, but the blond kid was kneeing the Italian in the groin while the other drover was hammering on the Italian's back with a rock. The Italian boy was crying out sharply every time the dukey crashed into his backbone, but he wasn't letting it interfere with stomping the drover's face. As Bricker hurried up, the Italian fell on top of the downed drover, the blond kid hit the other drover flush on the mouth, and the drover dropped his rock right onto his buddy's mid-section. This galvanized everybody into new activity and they crashed into each other, flailing away fist and foot and knee and elbow, everybody covered with torn clothes, dirt, sand, rocks, blood, snot, sweat, and some chicken manure they had rolled into someplace.

Standing in the doorway of Bricker's house, one arm around little Ellen (standing in a puddle) and her hand to her mouth, was Adele. She was wearing a simple skirt and a blouse with a neckline that plunged to the vicinity of the unmentionable. She looked sweet and young and sexy. And scared.

Bricker got the picture.

'All right,' he bawled, wading into the fight. 'That's it, break it up!'

The Italian yelled an obscenity and hit him in the mouth. The blond kid, attempting to hit one of the drovers, missed and hit Bricker on the back of the skull. Bright stars flashed and Bricker went to his knees. Somebody caved in on his back, flattening him, and a boot thudded into the side of his skull. For a split second he was out of it. *This is ridiculous*, he thought.

He got back to his feet. One of the drovers, blood flying from his smashed nose, threw a rock. Bricker caught his arm and swung him round and tripped him and kicked him in the belly as he fell. The Italian jumped on Bricker's back and Bricker gave him an elbow to the middle and a spur sharply on the instep, dropping him to his knees. Bricker locked his fists and swung them roundhouse, knocking the Italian back about five feet, tumbling. By this time, however, the other drover had crashed into Bricker in a flying tackle, and the blond kid, recognizing the common enemy, law and order, ran over with his favourite rock. A man could get killed this way, Bricker thought. He stuck his thumb into the drover's eye, swung an elbow, ducked the falling rock, tackled the blond kid, twisted his fingers backward, and chopped him across the Adam's apple. The kid went down. Bricker turned just in time to meet the on-charging drover, and bashed him between the eyes with the barrel of his Colt.

All of a sudden it had gotten very quiet.

Shaking from head to foot, Bricker surveyed the scene. One of the drovers sprawled in the dirt near the tree, still writhing from the groin-kick he had received. The other one lay face down, still retching although he was out cold. The Italian kid lay sprawled on his back, arms and legs wide, his blood-spattered face reflecting the sun. The blond boy had finished throwing up, but he knelt in the sand, one eye looking east and the other west, out of it.

Bricker turned to look at Adele. She stood trembling, her arm still around Ellen, the sunlight lovely and golden on the top halves of her full young breasts.

'Thank goodness you got here!' Adele gasped. 'It was so awful!'

'Awful?' Bricker repeated. 'Did you really think it was awful?'

'Of course! They were fighting, and—!'

'Adele,' Bricker said, controlling himself. 'Don't wear dresses that show quite so much. Not downtown anyway. Don't flirt with drovers you don't know. Don't flirt with *any* drovers. Don't bring 'em back here with you.'

'You're talking like a father,' Adele pouted. 'And you're hurting my feelings.'

'A couple of those boys might have been killed. *Killed.* Do you know what that means?'

Adele's eyes startled wide. 'I didn't realize—'

'*Start* realizing,' Bricker snapped, still angry because they had skirted so near senseless loss of life.

'I'm—sorry—'

'Okay,' Bricker said, relenting. 'Just . . . try.' He got up a smile for her. 'All right?'

'All right,' Adele said huskily.

The morning dragged. The temperature reached 100°. The colonel and his cronies were getting good and drunk. Bricket had a steak and fried potatoes and a slab of apple pie and two cups of coffee, and was feeling almost human again when he finished.

He was on his way towards the telegraph office, hoping for more wires and some real news on Wintle, when he turned a corner and nearly walked right into Billy Dean.

Dean's hair was standing on end and he was a little pale. He had Bobby Wintle with him, and when Bobby spotted Bricker, he literally jumped up and down and began dancing a jig.

'I did it!' Bobby chortled. 'I did it! Just like you said!' He pointed his index at Bricker. '*Pow!*'

Bricker at that point realized that the third man with them—a squatty, dirty, bearded, bedraggled, malodorous old gent with a crutch under one mangy armpit, was walking along in front of Billy Dean's levelled revolver. The old gent looked evilly at Bricker and didn't bat an eyelash.

'What's going on?' Bricker demanded.

'He did it, all right, boss,' Dean grinned. 'Just like he said, like you told him. Only they ran to get help, and they found me first. I got there, and there was Bobby, his finger in this old man's back, and the old man froze, I'm telling you, *froze*, just like it was a gun.'

Bricker's guts shrivelled. 'You didn't—?'

'It worked,' Bobby giggled, hopping again 'Pow! Pow! Pow! Pow!'

'And you arrested him,' Bricker said to Dean.

'He's a member of the Hash Knife Outfit,' Dean said happily.

'Who said?'

'Bobby said!'

'Oh, God,' Bricker said to himself.

'It was really, really neat!' Dean laughed.

Bricker steeled himself. He even closed his eyes for a moment. He looked at the old man. The old man glared right back, his gimpy leg supported by the crutch, which was wrapped with old bandages that looked like they had been used for every casualty in the war. The old man wasn't much over five feet tall, his pants were brown, his shirt blue and his coat sort of yellow. It was difficult to understand how one person of such small stature could carry so much dirt, but he managed. The wind stirred, and Bricker smelled buffalo, chicken manure, dead horse, whisky, tobacco, garlic, rotten eggs, old-man sweat, urine, alkali and something akin to rotten eggs.

'Who are you?' Bricker asked.

'Eat a fencepost,' the old man snarled.

He was probably president of the railroad, Bricker thought.

'If you don't identify yourself, we'll have to take you in,' Bricker said aloud.

'Of course we'll take him in!' Dean gasped. 'I told you, he's one of the Hash Knife Outfit!'

'Bite a pig,' the old man said. He seemed to have a one-track mind.

'All right,' Bricker said wearily. 'Let's go to jail.'

The old man, Bricker thought, was not a local, and he was a hardcase. He might also be a little drunk, but it was hard to tell, what with the bad leg and all. Chances were, he was drunk. And he would sober up. And sue the county for false arrest. Bricker realized that he should never have told Bobby Wintle to study the posters.

They reached the jail. They went in. Bobby ran to the desk and began madly shuffling through the neatly stacked posters and circulars. Dean shoved the old man with the gun in his back. 'Up against the wall!'

'Put your iron away,' Bricker snapped.

'He's dangerous,' Dean protested.

'Wait,' Bricker said. 'Think for a minute. *Think*. I know it's hard. Try. What are the odds against just walking down the street and spotting a member of the Hash Knife Outfit? What are the odds against this old man being a member of *any* self-respecting gang? What are the odds of fooling a real gunner with a finger in the back?'

Dean looked at him. Then he looked at the old man. Then he looked at his gun, and slowly holstered it. Then he looked at Bricker again.

'I didn't think,' he said.

Bricker took a deep breath.

'Here it is!' Bobby yelped, and ran from the desk.

He shoved the wanted poster at Bricker.

Bricker looked at it disgustedly. Then he looked at the old man.

And back at the poster. He began to tingle slightly.

Bobby was grinning at him. Dean, who had looked over his shoulder, began to grin, too. Bricker compared the photo and the old man once more. It was impossible.

SIMON FRINK, the poster said. $500 reward. Train robbery, suspicion of murder. A member of the Hash Knife Outfit.

Bricker looked at the old man. 'Simon Frink?' he breathed unbelievingly.

'Chew a snake,' the old man said.

It was him, all right.

Chapter Seven

Recovering from his initial shock, Adam Bricker figured it was no time to worry about his pride. He took long enough to build a couple of cigarettes, and lit one of them.

'Sit down,' he told Simon Frink.

Frink sat in the straight chair by the desk, bitterly staring into space. He had very few teeth. With his jaw set as it was now, his mouth just about vanished in the folds of flesh. He looked old and dirty and beat and angry and scroungy and trapped and harmless. Bricker felt a little sorry for him.

'Smoke?' Bricker asked, offering the other cigarette.

Frink glared at him, refusing.

'What are you doing in Hopewell?' Bricker asked, sitting behind the desk.

'Ain't sayin',' Frink grunted.

'Where's the rest of the gang?'

'Ain't sayin'.'

'I'll go easier on you if you cooperate.'

'Says you.'

Bobby Wintle stood back in the corner, eyes wide. But Billy Dean hopped nervously around, shuffling his feet and scratching his armpits. Bricker had known his deputy couldn't restrain himself long.

Dean fled, slamming the door behind him.

'Now,' Bricker said, turning back to Frink. 'You're a member of the Hash Knife Outfit. You can't deny that.'

Frink looked at him. Through the dirt and wrinkles it was hard to read the expression.

'You are a member,' Bricker said.

'Ain't sayin'.'

'How many in the gang now?'

'Huh-uh.'

'Where's the camp?'

'Nope.'

Frink ejected a stream of spittle between his gums and hit the general area of the wastebasket.

'You wouldn't have come in except for a purpose,' Bricker said. 'You knew you were running a chance.'

'Some chance,' Frink grunted. 'Nobody in the *world* reads them stupid circulars any more.'

Bricker chose to ignore this and what it implied. 'Somebody got hurt in the gang,' he guessed. 'You came for a doctor.'

Frink stared at him.

Bricker grabbed the front of his shirt and shook him, hard. He bellowed, 'We've got ways to beat it out of you, old man!'

Frink's toothless gums spread in a grin. 'Don't gimme that. Everybody knows Adam Bricker plays it straight down the middle. You might *wanna* beat on me, but you won't. See, that's where I got you, buddy. You're one of them play-fair, foller-the-law milk-toasters. And *I* ain't.'

Bricker took a deep breath and lit one cigarette off the butt of the other. 'All right,' he said quietly, amending his approach. 'Look at it this way. You're caught. You've had it. Why not make it easy on yourself? Nobody'll ever know you helped me.'

Frink looked bored again.

Bricker stamped out his fresh smoke. 'Okay, old man. In the cell.'

'Pleasure.' Frink smiled.

Bricker took him back and put him in the end compartment by himself. As the door clanged shut, Bricker told him, 'If you change your mind, give me a yell.'

'Not likely.'

Going back to the office, Bricker found Bobby Wintle still waiting.

'We sure did it, huh?' Bobby grinned.

Bricker patted him on the back. 'That we did, son.'

'Did he confess?'

'Not yet.'

'Boy, oh boy,' Bobby grinned.

'Maybe,' Bricker said, 'you ought to go back out and watch some more.'

'Yeah,' Bobby said, then said it more emphatically. 'Yeah! There might be more of 'em around, right?'

'Right,' Bricker said, forcing a smile. Wrong, he hoped. But he didn't feel as sure of himself as he had a little while ago.

Bobby scurried out, leaving the door ajar.

Bricker sat at his desk. It was mothering impossible. But Frink was a hardcase, all right, an old one, the toughest kind because you had to be really rugged, no matter how dumb you might look, to get past the age of fifty as an outlaw. A real toughie. And Bobby had caught him. Bricker looked at the wanted posters with a feeling of disbelief.

First, Simon Frink had been in town for *something*. It might mean the rest of the Hash Knife was close. Planning something in Hopewell? Maybe. Or a diversion? Or an accident?

It was a hard problem, one Bricker knew he couldn't solve without a confession from Frink. The old man was the *first* to be captured out of any of the three big gangs in the area.

And, Bricker realized with a start, a kid had done it, and this word would get around. Billy Dean probably was setting a world's record for indoor shooting off of the tonsils already. Everybody would hear about it.

Including Enright.

He was still thinking about it twenty minutes later when a horseman pounded up to the office porch.

'Sheriff! Sheriff!' he yelled, half-falling inside. 'The stage just got robbed by the Hole in the Wall Gang!'

Chapter Eight

Marshall drove the old flatbed wagon slowly into Hopewell. It was afternoon and the streets were crowded and it was scorchingly hot. No one paid any attention to Marshall as he guided the creaky wagon along past the depot, up a side street, onto Main, and down toward the bank corner. He congratulated himself.

Pulling the wagon over near the side of the street, Marshall set the hand brake and climbed down from the slab seat a half-block from tomorrow's target, the bank itself.

Across the street from the spot where Marshall parked, Clovis whanged Doreen with his elbow.

'Look over there!' Clovis breathed, his drowsiness forgotten.

'At what? Where?'

Clovis held his fist up to his chest and pointed with his thumb. 'There. Across the street, dummy.'

Doreen frowned into the hot glare. 'I don't see anything 'cept a dumb old wagon and a dumb farmer.'

'You just look closer,' Clovis said. Girls were so dumb!

The man across the street was just going into the hardware, so Clovis had to speak swiftly. '*Him*, ninny!'

'I don't see—'

'He's wearing overalls,' Clovis explained excitedly. 'Only he ain't no farmer. Look. He's got no patches on the knees, or on the elbows of that blue shirt, neither. And lookee at his boots. Those ain't work shoes, Doreen. Those are *riding* boots. See the heel on 'em? And they're not muddy or nothing. See that straw hat he's wearing? The brim is tore off in back,' Clovis explained. 'But his neck ain't sunburned back there. That means he don't ordinarily wear that hat at all.'

The man vanished into the hardware store.

'Who do you think he *is*?' Doreen asked, impressed.

'I don't know, but he's trying awful hard to make hisself look like a farmer, but he ain't.'

Doreen stood. 'Should I run get the sheriff?'

Clovis hesitated. Word had gotten to them about Bobby's capture of a genuine, living, breathing member of the Hash Knife Outfit. Clovis was *glad* about it of course. But he would have preferred the glory himself. Now the knot in his belly and the cooling of sweat on his back told him that his chance, too, was staring him right in the face. He didn't want to muff it—or call a false alarm.

'We'll watch awhile first,' he decided.

'You're not sure at all,' Doreen guessed.

Clovis tensed as the suspect came out of the hardware with a small keg of nails on his shoulder. The man walked to the back of the wagon and sat the keg down, brushed off his hands, and then shoved it back farther on the wagonbed, into the straw. The straw was pretty deep in the centre.

Clovis studied the man. He was young, curly haired, lightly athletic. Clovis would have liked to check his hands; he had read where Ned Buntline caught a fake farmer by feeling of his hands and finding no rough spots. Gunfighters didn't have rough spots, either. Clovis decided the man was a gunfighter posing as a farmer.

'He's probably a member of a gang,' he told Doreen.

Across the street, the man left the wagon and walked up the sidewalk toward the bank, his hands jammed in his pockets. He sauntered, really, whistling silently, gawking this way and that. When he reached the front of the bank, he paused and leaned way back and gawked up at the top of the structure as if it were the biggest, fanciest thing he had ever seen. But Clovis, watching like mad, made out the fact that the stranger was not really looking at the top of the building at all; his head was pointed *up*, but his eyeballs were staring hard right straight *in*, through the front doors.

Clovis didn't even mention this to Doreen, who was pouting again. He was beginning to sweat profusely with tingling excitement. He was right, he was right, he was right! The guy *was* an outlaw of some kind!

The stranger stopped gawking and strolled around the bank corner, out of sight.

He was, Clovis thought, going down the side street to get another view in through a window of the bank. *And to see the back door.*

He was a bank robber in disguise!

Had to be. No other explanation. Couldn't be a rube looking the town over, or a new farmer who hadn't had time to wear holes in his clothes yet, or a cowboy who got in some manure and wore the next best thing, or a drover who gambled away his horse and was stuck with the wagon, or a drifter killing time. Had to be a bank robber in disguise. Clovis had secretly read enough dime novels to *know* that the obvious was never correct, that you had to look for these little clues.

Clovis told his sister, 'I think we'd better go find the sheriff now.'

'You tell him this stuff you told me,' Doreen said, 'and he's really going to think you're dumb, Clovis.'

Clovis held back the hot retort. He wondered if his sister might not have a point. After all, he was not absolutely sure.

But he had to do something and he had to do it pretty fast. The bank robber in disguise would be back in a minute, Clovis was sure of that. Then he would just ride out of town to the gulch where thirty or forty other tough, mean hombres were waiting on their big black horses, and they would come in and kill everybody and take the money and blow up the train and all. Clovis had to act *right now*.

As he thought about it, sweat dripping into his eyes with salt sting, the stranger came ambling back around the corner, headed toward his wagon again.

Clovis's insides dropped in shocked disappointment. He watched, horrified, as the stranger walked along, hands still in his pockets, passing the bank again, and the feed store, and the livery, headed for the wagon. Clovis knew sickeningly he had blown it, he should have moved sooner, the stranger was going to head straight out.

The stranger walked up to the wagon, glanced

around, and stood for a moment. Clovis watched so hard his eyeballs ached. He could see the Bull Durham sack strings in the boob's pocket and his two-day growth of beard and the way his eyes were darting around, taking everything in.

Then, startled, he saw the stranger turn his back on the wagon. The stranger turned and walked up the street and went into a saloon.

The moment he was out of sight, Clovis bashed Doreen with his elbow again.

'*Dang* it, Clovis—!' Doreen gasped in pain.

'C'mon,' Clovis muttered, scrambling to his feet.

On legs tingly from squatting too long, Clovis scurried across the street. Some riders humped by, stirring up billows of choking yellow-red dust, and everybody up and down the street turned away from the wind-scoured cloud for an instant. It was in this instant that Clovis formalized his Big Idea, and got to the wagon. Using the side back wheel as a ladder, he climbed up inside.

'What are you doing?' Doreen squealed.

'Listen,' Clovis told her peering down from the straw pile. 'I gotta follow this guy. It's my big chance. You go back home and don't say *nothing* to *nobody*, you understand?'

'They'll say, "Where did Clovis go?"' Doreen protested as the heavy dust swirled around them.

Clovis burrowed into the straw, burying himself. He got it arranged so that he was hidden except for his head. 'You don't know *nothing*,' he said sternly. 'This is important, Sis.'

The scene was a point beyond Ham Mesa where the stage road dipped into an ancient depression where once there had been a sweet water hole. Now only a few scrubby blackjacks stood against the high, hot wind, and dust blew. In the road stood the stage, and under the trees stood Adam Bricker, the driver, the shotgun man, and the three passengers: an elderly nun, a fat drummer, and a beat-up old cowboy.

Bricker mopped sweat from his brow, licked the stump of his pencil, and smudged notes into a small booklet. 'The way I see it, then,' he said, 'they hid in this gully and came out when you got here.'

The driver pointed phlegmatically. 'Right down there, yep.'

'No one hurt?'

The people looked at each other. The nun crossed herself. 'Praise be to God,' she said.

'How many people?' Bricker asked.

'Three,' the driver said, spitting expertly at a stump.

'The Hole in the Wall Gang,' the shotgun man added.

Bricker looked at him. 'The Hole in the Wall Gang is bigger than that.'

'I seen Fred Green once, and Fred Green was one of 'em.'

Bricker frowned and made notes. 'You didn't see any other men hiding around nearby?'

'Nope. Just them three.'

'What did they get?' he asked.

'No money box,' the driver grunted. 'I had four dollars.'

'They took my watch,' the shotgun man added.

76

Bricker looked at the passengers.

'I lost my watch and a gold chain worth more than fifty dollars,' the drummer said. 'They broke open my sample case, but as I deal in soap and shaving lotions, they didn't take it.'

Bricker glanced at the nun. She returned his gaze, and then tears appeared in her eyes. 'I had a rosary, a very precious one. It—it included a relic of the True Cross.'

'They took that?'

'Yes.'

'Anything else?'

'It was my most precious thing!'

'I'm sorry,' Bricker said sincerely. He turned to the old cowboy who had been drinking before the robbery, or after. Or both. 'How about you?'

'They took my gun,' the grizzled redhead muttered, swaying. 'Worth thirty, forty dollars. A fine piece. And my watch. It was a hunnert dollar watch. It was real valuable, Sheriff, I ain't kidding.'

'I'm sure it was,' Bricker said. 'I hope we can recover it. Now I suggest, unless anyone has anything to add to this report, you go ahead and get this stage into town, Barney.'

The driver nodded and started for the stage, but the cowboy yelped. 'Don't brush me off, Sheriff! I'm a citizen! I got rights! What're you gonna do about my precious watch them guys stole? Has this company got insurance? I demand to be paid!'

'Take it up with the stage line office,' Bricker suggested looking around in the loose dirt for sign.

'Listen,' the cowboy bawled. 'You're takin' this

awful light! I've heard how you can't catch these fellers! Don't think you're gonna mess around with me, buster, because—*awrk!*'

Bricker had reached over and grabbed the front of his shirt and now held him pinioned against the nearest tree, his feet dangling off the ground a good six inches.

'What did you say?' Bricker snapped.

'Nothing!' the cowboy gasped, choking. 'I was funnin', Sheriff!' He managed a ghastly grin. 'See? Heh-heh.'

Bricker let him down. 'All right.'

The cowboy hustled off for the stage. The shotgun man, hiding his grin, climbed up beside the driver. The nun and the drummer got in. The doors closed. '*Hyar!*' the driver yelled, and the team pulled off strongly, pluming up dust.

Bricker stood in the roadway, letting the gunk sift down out of the air upon him. It stuck because he was soaked with sweat. He watched the stage go through the low area and then climb, creaking and swaying, up onto the flat road again, and high-tail toward town.

Back in Hopewell, Bricker barned his animal and limped toward home. The sun was slanting far into the west, and if you tried hard enough, you could convince yourself it was cooler.

He was halfway down the block toward his office when he met U. S. Bagwell, the saloon owner, coming the other way. Bagwell looked tired, and his face glistened with sweat.

'I was looking for you,' Bagwell said.

'What's going on?' Bricker asked.

'Well, nothing yet, Adam. But that damned colonel is still in my place. He's been drinking more beer than I thought any six men could hold down. He keeps making these speeches, and lately he's been getting pretty raw, even for my place. I'm afraid he'll make somebody mad if he keeps it up.'

'Do you want him out of there?' Bricker asked.

Bagwell mopped his face. 'Well . . . I wouldn't go that far, not yet, anyway. I'm just worried, that's all.'

'Has Billy Dean been around?'

'He's been in and out all afternoon. Last time, though, the colonel noticed his badge and started insulting *him*, real bad. Billy left, and now he's just sort of walking up and down the streets, going by now and then.'

It sounded like his deputy was using his head for once. 'Okay, buddy. I'll keep an eye out myself, and you let us know if it starts looking bad.'

Bagwell nodded, worried.

Bricker started on.

At the office, he checked his prisoners and found everything in order. While he was washing up, Adele came in. She was wearing a modest brown dress, and looked radiant as usual despite a line of worry across her forehead.

'We'll be ready to eat any time,' she told him.

'I'll be right back there, then,' Bricker decided. He was stripped to the waist and towelling himself.

She turned and started for the door.

'You worried about something?' Bricker asked.

She turned back. 'Clovis. He's—gone off someplace.'

'Where?' Bricker asked.

'That's just it. I don't know. I suppose the little scamp just walked outside town, or found another boy to play with somewhere, but he hasn't been around since lunchtime, and I'm getting worried.'

'He probably found another kid,' Bricker guessed. 'He'll turn up soon. His belly will be getting empty.'

Adele sighed. 'I suppose so.'

'Go on back to the house,' he said huskily. 'I'll be back soon, and we can eat. Clovis will show up, if I know kids.'

Bricker took his place at the table with a sense of thankfulness. He watched Adele. She was so much younger, he could watch her with a real sense of distance. He found himself translating her movements, and her slight humming, into pictures of Helen Jefferson. If he had better prospects, maybe he could ask Helen to marry him. It was *right*, having a woman around. He and Helen. . . .

He forced himself to stop thinking about it.

Everyone sat down.

'That Clovis,' Adele murmured, frowning.

'He'll show up,' Bricker said confidently.

But by 6.30, there was still no Clovis. Bricker left the house and went back to the office, where he met Billy Dean to get a routine report. Hopewell was filling up, and tomorrow would be worse, a real wing-ding for the local bartenders.

'We'll try not to jail anybody we don't have to,' Bricker decided. 'Carry a shotgun tonight and try to intimidate people.'

'What's intimidate mean?' Billy Dean asked, blank.

'Scare the liver out of them.'

'Oh. Sure.'

It got dark. An Irishman and a Methodist got in a knife fight behind the Baptist church, and Bricker had to knock heads and jail the both of them. A small riot in Slim's Howdy-Do Club was put down by a shotgun blast into the ceiling. The colonel managed, by dint of heroic effort, to insult a bar girl at Bagwell's. The girl tried to shoot him. Bricker unceremoniously knocked her on the head and told Bagwell to put her to bed for the night, and lock her in.

It got to be nine o'clock, and Bricker was busy running from one brush fire to the next. He forgot all about Clovis.

Then Bobby Wintle caught up with him in the Blue Note.

'He's still missing,' Bobby said, worried.

'Who?' Bricker said.

'Clovis.'

Bricker remembered. He consulted his pocket watch. It was almost ten o'clock. In the din and chaos of the saloon crowd, Bricker thought about it. He felt real worry now.

'Nobody's seen him?' he asked.

'No sir,' Bobby said, pale.

Bricker looked around the crowd. He spotted Young, the livery man. He pushed through. 'Bill?' he yelled over the noise.

'Yeah!' Young turned, pie-eyed.

'We've got a missing kid,' Bricker shouted. 'Can you help us look for him?'

Young made a face. 'Don't you think I'm too drunk?'

Bricker considered it. 'Yes,' he had to admit.

He went back to Bobby Wintle. 'Go find Dean. Tell him we need six or eight men to be a search party for Clovis.'

'Do you think—' Bobby began.

'No, I don't think *anything*. But I figure Clovis walked off someplace and maybe even fell in a hole and hurt his leg or something, and it's time we hunt around town and pick him up and take him home so I can beat his rear for him.'

Bobby nodded, almost smiled, and pressed out through the crowd.

Bricker left the saloon moments later. He was more concerned than he had let Bobby know. And of course it had to happen on Friday night, when things were at their worst.

He started looking for men to help in the search.

By 10.30, Bricker had exactly five men out looking. He had asked fifty.

Chapter Nine

False dawn leaked purple across the sky. Amos Tucker rolled out of his blanket, sat up, blinked painfully at the desolate wasteland stretching vacantly in all directions, scratched fiercely in his armpit, located a flea, and crushed it expertly between the nails of his thumb and index finger.

He turned, scratching some more, and blinked at the other bedroll. The figure in the roll hadn't stirred.

'Theodore,' Amos said huskily.

No response.

Amos went over and kicked the sleeping figure. It erupted into wild contortions, arms and legs flying, dirt being kicked around. Out of the blankets poked a bald head, a round face with moon-like eyes, and then a skinny naked torso with old-man teats dark beneath thin grey body hair.

'Git up, Theodore,' Amos said.

'You kick me once too often, Amos,' the other man grunted, 'and I might kill you.' The words were rubbery and muffled.

'Put your teeth in, stupid,' Amos said. 'I can't even savvy what you're sayin'.'

Theodore, sitting naked in his blankets, reached to his shirt and pants on the ground nearby. Fishing in a pocket of the shirt, he got out his store-bought teeth and shoved them into his face. They clicked loudly into place. 'I said—'

'I know what you said. Git outta there.'

Theodore complied, pulling on his pants and shirt.

'Simon come back?' Theodore asked.

Amos built a small pyramid with tiny sticks for a smokeless fire. 'Course not. We both know what happened by now. He got hisself arrested.'

'Well,' Theodore said, 'that makes me real mad. We ain't done nothing.'

'We're the Hash Knife Outfit,' Amos pointed out with some pride.

'We *was*,' Theodore corrected him bitterly.

'We're still it. We're all that's left.'

'When Brady and Younger and Stevens and Blount left, the Hash Knife died, Amos. You and me and Simon, we're all that's left. And the three of us ain't worth a hoot.'

'We're still the Hash Knife,' Amos insisted.

'Three old boys that started running together in Brown's Hole when we was dodging the draft,' Theodore said wearily. 'Some gang *we* are. The most we've stole the last four months is a chicken. We don't even have enough money to buy bullets, if we *did* want to rob something.'

Amos got the fire started with only the slightest wisp of smoke. He put the water on to boil. 'We might not be much, Theodore, but you've saw the papers.

They're still scared of us, boy. And now they've gone and arrested Simon.'

'You really think so?' Theodore asked.

'We don't haf to let 'em take Simon without a fight.'

Theodore stared at him. 'Huh?'

'I mean,' Amos said, warming to his topic, 'we can make 'em sorry they messed with the Hash Knife!'

'How?' Theodore asked.

'By gawd,' Amos blustered, the whisky talking for him, 'we can go in that there town and bust Simon out—and rob their dadgum bank for 'em while we're at it! Put the fear of the Lord in 'em!'

'Us?' Theodore asked blankly. 'You an' me?'

'We're the Hash Knife,' Amos pointed out once more with simple dignity.

'We,' Theodore countered, 'are a couple of stove-up ole—'

'You got no guts?' Amos flared.

'I got guts I ain't used yet! Speak for yourself!'

'All right, then,' Amos snapped. 'Let's jus' say we'll go in there today and rob their bank, and then in the confusion we'll bust Simon out. What do you say to that?'

Wide-eyed, Theodore tugged at the bottle again. He handed it over. He rocked on his haunches. Now, Amos thought, Theodore would talk him out of it. Good.

'I don't even know,' Theodore said thoughtfully, 'if my hoss can go that far. He's got rheumatism awful bad.'

'Okay,' Amos sneered. 'Forget it.'

'No,' Theodore said suddenly. 'I'll *make* the hoss go

that far—and while we're stealin' everything else, we'll steal me a new hoss, too!'

Amos was jolted. 'You wanna do it?'

'We're the Hash Knife, like you said!' Theodore's eyes were alive now. 'We can set out here an' hide, an' our bones fall apart, an' slobbers run down our face—or we can *do* somepin. An' you know what *I* think, Amos? By gawd, I think we're gonna do it, jus' like you said! We're gonna be the Hash Knife again, an' git ole Simon out, too!'

The Hash Knife *was* going to ride again.

Adam Bricker felt out on his feet. The light of dawn hurt his eyes as he trudged back toward his office. First day-time gusts of wind scattered bits of trash along the deserted streets of Hopewell, adding somehow to Bricker's feeling of desolation.

Near his office he met Harold Enright walking in the other direction. The newspaper publisher looked brisk and wide awake. He saluted with his cane. 'Good morning, Sheriff! Up bright and early, I see!'

'Haven't been to bed,' Bricker said thickly.

Enright frowned. 'You haven't found the boy?'

'We haven't,' Bricker bit off, 'and after all night of begging people to help, I've still got exactly nine men helping me look.'

'That's not a very goodly number,' Enright said dubiously.

'The kid got himself in some kind of trouble,' Bricker said, his anger a dull edge against his brain. 'Maybe somebody took him. Maybe he wandered off and got lost or fell in a well. I don't know. But he would have been back. He's in trouble. We have to find him. And in this whole God-forsaken, rotten little town, there are just nine men who care enough to help me hunt for him.'

'You're angry,' Enright said.

'I'm angry,' Bricker snapped. 'I'm angry. Yeah. And I'm sick of the gutless cowards around here who talk a good game and won't help.'

'Well, now, Sheriff, you may be too hard on people. Everyone is busy with his own affairs—'

'And a little old kid may be dying someplace, but they have to tend to their own knitting and not get involved. Right!'

'There's no call to shout at me,' Enright gasped. 'If it weren't for my duties with the paper, you know I'd help!'

'You probably would,' Bricker admitted bitterly. 'But most of these people wouldn't. And pardon me, but right now I'm real busy hating their guts for it.'

'Where are your men searching now?'

'We finished town,' Bricker explained. 'I've sent one group out on the west road, and another group east. Billy Dean got a couple of hours' sleep, and in a little while he'll ride out and check with each group to see if they've found any sign.'

'And you?'

'I'm going to sleep an hour. Got to.'

'You look like you need it.'

'Yeah,' Bricker muttered, and walked on towards his office.

He knew it was wrong to feel this kind of hate. Most of the men were good men; they would have helped if they could. Their exuses were good excuses *to them*. He shouldn't blame them.

But he did blame them. They were quick enough to carp when a crime went unsolved, eager enough to cackle at Enright's shafts in the paper. But give them a request for help—not for your own sake but for a *kid's*— and they could find excuses.

Scared half out of his wits and lashed to the wheel of the wagon, Clovis sat in the dirt of the campsite, watching the gang members break camp. It was shortly after dawn.

The four members of the Stillwell Mob had been as surprised by the capture yesterday as Clovis had been. He had been congratulating himself all the way back, hiding under the straw in the back of the wagon, bouncing around a bit, but riding comfortably. When the stranger finally reined up after a three-hour ride, Clovis had known he was onto something big. He had huddled in the straw and listened to the conflab:

'*Everything go all right?*'

'*Fine, boss. No hitches at all.*'

'*How does it look?*'

'*Looks good. Main Street is okay for getaway. I've got a paper marked here with the way we can go in, using the back streets, and then the alley. There's a steel door on the back, but we can bust it.*'

'*How about Bricker?*'

'*Didn't see him.*'

'*All right. Git down. We'll run this rig you stole down into the gully where nobody'll find it for months.*'

Digesting this information, Clovis huddled under the

straw while listening to sounds of the team being unhitched and things moved around. Several men's voices muttered. He waited.

Then someone said, '*Altogether, now. Give it a good shove and it'll go over the brink.*'

Only then had Clovis realized that they were preparing to roll the wagon over a cliff or something—with him on it. He knew he would be discovered if he moved. But panic took hold. He jumped.

He rolled out of the wagon and right into the midst of the four startled desperadoes. He tried to break through them—the campsite was on the edge of woods and beside a deep, tree-filled gully, and he imagined for one delightful split-second that he could make it and get away—but then someone yelled hoarsely and someone else banged him alongside the head, and he went down sprawling, tasting his own blood.

'Set on him!' somebody yelled.

'Who is he?' someone else shouted, sitting on Clovis.

And that, as they said, had been all she wrote.

Oh, Clovis had maintained his composure, more or less. He knew right off that they were a bad gang, for real. They talked tough, and he knew they might kill him, but he figured his only chance was to lie, so he did. He told them he thought it was his daddy's wagon, and he curled up in the back to go to sleep, and woke up just a minute ago. The big dark man, the one they called 'boss', said he was a lousy little liar. But Clovis stammered and sniffled and clung to his lousy little lie.

Finally, they had tied him up and ignored him.

Now the four of them were breaking camp, obviously. The one who had come to town dressed like a farmer—

his real name, Clovis had figured out, was Marshall —
was packing saddlebags and helping another of the
men, a flat-faced one named Jersey Jack, with saddling.
The one Clovis *knew*, in his guts, was a real killer, the
one named Dan Harp, was tidying up the area. The
boss—Fred Stillwell—hunkered over a folded-out
sheet of paper near what had been the campfire.

'We'll ride out around to the north, and go in from
the opposite side,' he told his men. 'We've got plenty of
time.'

'We still hit it right at two?' Harp asked.

'Right. Does everybody understand exactly what the
plan is?'

The three men stood around the boss and nodded
soberly. 'Questions?' Stillwell asked, looking at them in
turn.

Harp, the gunman, glanced toward Clovis. 'How
about him?'

Stillwell scowled. 'I've been trying to make up my
mind.'

Harp said, 'We got to kill him. He can identify us.'

'I don't hold with killing babies.'

'We got no choice.'

Stillwell got to his feet, walked over, and looked down
at Clovis. 'You're a problem, boy.'

Clovis couldn't possibly say anything because there
was something big and sour stuck in his throat. *Kill*
him? Good cow, he was too young to die! He didn't
want to die!

'It has to be done,' Harp said impassively, his eyes
like a snake's.

No one spoke.

'I'll do it,' Harp offered.

Marshall said huskily, 'I don't like it either, but what's the option?'

Stillwell frowned more deeply. 'Jack?'

The old fighter swayed back and forth. Finally he rumbled, 'Guess we godda, boss.' He seemed sad about it.

Stillwell looked down at Clovis again. Stillwell was a rugged man, and a mean one. But did Clovis only imagine a flutter of sympathy somewhere back behind those dark, bitter eyes?

'Untie him,' Stillwell said abruptly. 'We'll shove the wagon into the gulch. We should have done that yesterday already, the way we started to. Then we'll deal with the kid.'

Without a word, Harp came forward with a wicked bowie knife. Clovis flinched, but the blade only snicked through the ropes. Harp hauled him roughly to his feet.

'I'll hold him,' Stillwell muttered, taking Clovis's arm. 'The three of you shove that wagon over.' As he spoke, Stillwell dragged him away from the wagon and into the middle of the campsite, a few feet from the weed-choked rim of the drop-off into the gully. It was weedy, woody and messy down there, tangled with creepers and dense vegetation. The camp, on its edge, had been well-hidden.

Stillwell's hand around his arm was like a vice. 'Shove it over,' Stillwell ordered.

The three men got behind the flatbed wagon and gave a heave. The wagon groaned and stayed stuck.

'More,' Marshall grunted, finding a better place to put his shoulder.

They shoved again, faces contorting. The wagon lurched and rolled forward ponderously, its front wheels perching on the weedy edge of the drop-off.

Stillwell whispered fiercely, so only Clovis could hear: '*I'm letting you go, boy. I don't cotton to killing younguns. Run for it—if we catch you, you're dead.*'

The whisper barely reached Clovis's ears because of the racket the wagon was making as it lurched over the brink of the precipice and began to tumble down the other side, thrashing and crashing brush as it picked up momentum. All three of the other men were standing there, watching it go for an instant. Clovis thought maybe he was hearing things, because Stillwell's big fist still held his arm tightly. *Oh grannies I'm crazy, I'm hearing things, I'm dead*, Clovis thought wildly.

Then Stillwell's grip relaxed.

'*Go!*' Stillwell hissed.

Clovis froze. Go where?

The woods behind him? The open weeds out yonder? The precipice that the wagon was thundering and crashing down into with enormous racket? He didn't know which way to go. It was too sudden, too unexpected, and his legs and arms were weak with fright, and he felt like he was going to puke again with fright—and—

—*and:* the three men were beginning to turn away from the spectacle of the wagon crashing out of sight.

He had to go *now*.

Wrenching out of Stillwell's relaxed grip, he spun toward the weedy brink of the deep gully.

'Hey!' Stillwell roared, as if shocked and angry.

'Stop him!' somebody else yelled.

Then bodies were moving and shouts shouting, but Clovis didn't see or hear it too much because he had gone head-first over the brink of the gully, tearing through weeds and stickers, falling free for a long, sickening moment, hitting, bouncing, falling through more brush. And then he was tumbling head-over-heels, wildly, down through brush and stickers, down the side of the nearly perpendicular wall of the gully, and somewhere back overhead, a gun boomed, and he was still bouncing down crazily.

Chapter Ten

'Adam?' The voice was soft, and then more insistent, worried.

'*Adam?*'

Bricker hauled himself back from the great soft deeps of sleep. It hurt to come back so soon. Opening his eyes, he was disoriented and jangled.

Adele, pink and pretty in a soft blue housedress, was bending over him with a worried frown. Behind her stood someone else; Bricker got the other figure in focus. Helen Jefferson.

'Someone is here to see you,' Adele murmured, her hand on his shoulder.

'What time is it?' His voice croaked.

'Almost ten.'

'Damn!' He got to his feet. 'Hello, Helen.'

Helen wore a dark summer frock and a bonnet, but her eyebrows were knit in a frown as if she were fighting a glare. 'Hello, Adam.'

'What's going on?'

Before Helen could reply, Adele fussed at Bricker's shirt buttons, tidying him up, and stood on tip-toes to brush his hair back for him. 'Can I get the two of you coffee? You poor thing, you still look so tired!'

Flustered, Bricker pushed Adele's hands away. 'You want some coffee, Helen?' he asked.

Helen's voice would have frozen a hot water bottle. 'Not here, thank you.'

Bricker shook himself. 'You uh want to go to the café?'

'Yes,' Helen bit off just as icily.

She was mad. Why? Bricker was still fuzzy in the skull from sleep. He reached for his gunbelt, strapped it back on, and got his hat. 'Okay. We'll go to the café.'

Adele stepped back obediently, watching him with big, worshipful eyes. From the kitchen, Doreen and little Ellen came into the room.

'Scat!' Adele told them. 'I told you Adam needs his rest!'

'I'm awake now,' Bricker grunted. 'Hello, kids.'

Ellen looked up at him and stuck her thumb in her mouth. Doreen appeared almost as stricken. 'Have they found Clovis yet?' she asked.

'Not yet,' Bricker said, 'as far as I know. I expect Bobby would have been right in here to tell us if they had. He's with one group and my deputy is with the other, so no news is bad news in this case.'

'Do you think Clovis is dead?' Doreen asked.

'Of course not!' Bricker said sharply. 'What makes you think a thing like that?'

Doreen frowned. 'Nothing.'

'He just wandered off,' Bricker said.

'Yes,' Doreen said. 'But . . .' Her voice trailed off.

'But what?' Bricker asked.

Doreen evidently thought better of whatever she had started to say. 'Nothing,' she murmured.

Feeling sorry for the tyke, Bricker tousled her hair. He told Adele, 'I'll check back after a while. Keep these kids close. One lost one is enough.'

'Yes, Adam,' Adele breathed.

'Come on, Helen,' Bricker said, leading her to the door.

'You be careful, now,' Adele called after him.

Bricker waved and took Helen outside. The sun was high and blasting hot. The glare sank all the way through his skull and hit like melted lead against the back, sliding painfully down his spine. He limped along with Helen at his side as they crossed the weedy yard, skirted the jail, and went into the street, heading for the café.

'What's on your mind?' Bricker asked her.

Helen kept her eyes straight ahead and her lips pursed. 'Nothing.'

Helen said nothing, and marched along at a pace that would have strained an infantryman.

'You came and woke me,' Bricker pointed out.

'I'm sorry,' Helen bit off. 'Next time I won't bother you.'

'I needed to get up. What I meant was, you must have wanted *something*.'

'I'm sure I did,' Helen said, adding with acid sarcasm-sweetness, 'Adam.'

'What are you so steamed up about?'

'Nothing,' she spat, eyes still straight ahead.

'Was I supposed to come see you or something?' he asked.

'Certainly not, *Adam*,' Helen replied with the same biting sarcasm. 'Just so you be *careful*, now, hon, you'all hear?' She shot him a withering look and added a flip of her hands—decidedly uncharacteristic of her, but a perfect, if destructive, imitation of Adele. 'You jus' be *careful*,' she added, every word dripping venomous, gooey imitation.

'You're mad about Adele!' Bricker grinned, tumbling.

'Why should I be?' Helen fired back, her eyes sizzling. 'If you want to tippy-toe around with a little fluff like that, acting like a stupid idiot while she flusters and picks and smoothes and pats you, it's none of *my* business!'

'You *are*,' Bricker gasped. 'Hey, you don't think that little girl and I—you don't think I'd—'

'It makes no difference what I might think,' Helen snapped. 'Obviously.'

'Helen! She's *seventeen*! I'm—'

'A man,' Helen supplied, still stalking along.

'I'm just taking care of her and the other kids! She's—'

'Don't tell me you don't like it!' Helen hissed, whirling to face him with the fury of a tigress. She stabbed at his chest with a finger. 'I come over *worried* about you, thinking you need help or something, and what do I find? *What* . . . *do* . . . *I* . . . *find?* You there asleep, and that brazen little hussy sitting there in the next chair, watching you like a little mother! Do you know she wasn't going to wake you for me until I practically told her I'd scratch her eyes out? Well, all right, Adam Bricker! I won't bother you again! I've been a fool, all right, but even a fool can learn! You can just take your life and—and *jump in the river*!'

'What river?' Bricker choked.

'Oh,' Helen spluttered. 'You—you big—you big—*fool*!'

She turned and stormed off.

'Helen!' Bricker called, so loudly that people turned to look.

She kept right on going, and out of sight into a store.

Bricker stood rooted for a moment, shock mixed with awareness that people were staring and grinning. Then, his face feeling hot, he turned and stomped on down the street toward the café.

She was mad. *Really* mad. He hadn't expected it because—because why? His ears were still tingling, but as he strode along, an idea began dawning that made him feel better.

She was mad *because she was jealous*. And to be jealous, boys, you've got to like somebody. A whole lot. Suddenly Bricker chuckled aloud.

Still thinking about it with mixed surprise and growing pleasure, he went into the café. It was late for breakfast, and a couple of men sat at one table having coffee. Beside the counter stood one person Bricker didn't mind seeing, Mayor Steed, and one he did, Colonel T. T. Clydesdale.

'There comes yon sheriff this very moment,' the colonel intoned, brandishing his cane in Bricker's direction. 'We can ascertain the facts of the situation without further delay or dilemma.'

Bricker braced himself inwardly and walked over. Morning, Mayor.'

'Good morning,' Steed murmured, looking glum.

The colonel tapped him on the chest with the head of the cane. 'Tell me, my good man, what is the status of the missing little beast?'

'Still missing,' Bricker said, signalling the waiter for coffee.

'Too bad, too bad,' the colonel monotoned.

'We have all the men out who are willing to help.'

'Yes,' the colonel said. 'Indeed. Very well, then, Sheriff. You may carry on.'

'Speaking of carrying on,' Bricker said, 'you owe quite a bill for that broken glass last night at Carrie's place.'

'I was not myself,' the colonel countered. 'Knowing that my young secretary and companion was awaiting my company, I would not have ventured into Carrie's establishment if I had not been rendered momentarily mad by a combination of heat and dust.'

'You broke six mirrors.'

'Yes, so I did, so I did. I trust my quota of bad luck will be served concurrently. If the term is established on a consecutive basis, I may never hold another royal flush as long as I live.'

'You'll take care of the bill?' Bricker prodded.

'Indeed, indeed. Think no more of it. I shall endeavour to set matters aright the instant I have completed my duties with the bank today.'

'Fine,' Bricker said. His coffee came.

At the house behind the jail, Doreen sat in the yard with

Ellen and watched her play in the sand. Doreen was really, really scared.

She knew Clovis had been captured. Nothing else would account for it. He had gone out with that man, and that man had caught him. Now Clovis was in bad, bad trouble.

She really ought to tell someone what she knew, she thought.

But Clovis had told her to inform *no one*.

Maybe if she waited just a *little* longer, the situation would clarify itself.

Doreen decided she would wait.

Chapter Eleven

The camp had been struck. Horses stood ready under the blazing sun. The men hunkered against bleached rocks. Tommy Delbert was methodically checking the loads in his revolver again and Donnie Hawkins stared into space. Green and Simms frowned at their feet.

Preacher Addison took out his watch. 'Jeff,' he decided, 'start.'

Jeff Simms nodded and got to his feet. He took out his watch. 'I got ten-thirty on the nose.'

Addison wound his timepiece again. 'Right.' He looked around. 'Everybody got that?'

Other watches came out. The men made adjustments.

'We got to move together,' Addison reminded them. 'The time is important.'

'Right at two,' Addison reminded Simms. 'You start down from the saloon. You'll see all of us moving, too.'

Simms nodded and walked to his horse. He checked straps, then swung into the saddle. Leather creaked. He turned his mount and headed out, walking at first, then breaking into a gallop.

Addison and his remaining men watched the horseman become a speck, then a distant smudge of dust on the way toward Hopewell. No one spoke.

They were all nervous, Addison thought. But they were good men despite their youth. They would do fine.

No one would be expecting a robbery, Addison reflected, and the timing, if right, would make it almost easy.

He was still a little worried about Adam Bricker. But Bricker was the chance they had to take. There would never be a better time than now, with Bricker busy looking after those kids.

It would be the Hole in the Wall Gang's finest hour.

Some time passed in silence. Addison and his men hunkered and sweated.

Addison took out his watch again. It was almost eleven.

'Tommy,' he told Tommy Delbert, 'go.'

Delbert uncoiled lazily, hitched up his belt, grinned tautly, and walked to his horse. He mounted.

'See you in Hopewell,' he said softly.

'Yeah,' Addison grunted.

Delbert rode out, following the same general line taken by Simms.

Addison, Green, and Hawkins remained. Hawkins built a smoke, broke the paper, cursed softly, and started again.

Nerves were fine, Addison thought forgivingly. Nerves would make him function more sharply in town. It was going to be fine; they were right on schedule, and all that money was waiting.

At two o'clock it would be all theirs.

'Man,' Theodore Oglevie said disgustedly, 'this old nag ain't gonna make it.'

Amos Tucker looked at his partner, whose mount was so swaybacked he looked like two sliding boards bolted in the middle. 'He'll make it, don't worry.'

Theodore spat. 'It's after eleven already.'

'He'll make it,' Amos said. 'We'll make it.' He reached up and reassuringly touched the railroad detective badge pinned on the front of his undershirt, right beside his suspenders. 'We got it made, Theodore. We got a good plan and we got plenty of time and we're gonna do fine.'

'I jus' wish we had more bullets.'

'We'll make it,' Amos soothed him.

And it was funny: Amos *knew* now that they really would. The badges, dug out of the ruck hidden from an ancient train job, had been the last stroke of genius he had needed to reassure himself. They would walk in, the badges looked real official, nobody would be on guard for a minute, they would say they were train dicks and they needed to check security precautions, and by the time somebody tumbled, Theodore would have his gun on the guard and he would be inside the vault, shovelling the gold into bags.

Nobody had to know they didn't have enough bullets between them to load one gun. It would *work*.

The old Hash Knife was riding again.

Running ahead of him in the deep brush, Jersey Jack tripped over a downed log and ploughed head-first into a mudhole. Fred Stillwell pulled up short and leaned, panting raggedly, against a mossy tree.

'Hold it, hold it,' he gasped.

Jersey Jack scrambled wildly to his feet, a mud-covered lump. 'Godda ged him,' he panted.

It got quiet around them, in the green, with trees overhead and weeds and brush all around, rocks sticking out of ravine walls, a creek underfoot. Leaning heavily against the tree, his legs dead with fatigue, Stillwell listened to distant sounds, and placed his other men by them. Off to the left somewhere: a continuous thrashing, clattering of rocks and muffled curses: Marshall fighting his way through the deep briars and creepers infesting the left slope. Off to the right, and above: sliding pebbles and rocks coming down as Dan Harp scrambled madly along the cliff face, trying to see ahead.

Stillwell made some decisions. cupped his hands at his mouth, and bellowed: '*All right, boys! Come on down!*'

The thrashing and cursing paused on the left. Marshall's voice came raggedly, '*What?*'

'Come on over this way!'

Up above, more pebbles tumbled.

'*Harp!*' Stillwell bellowed.

The sounds stopped.

'*Come on down here!*' Stillwell yelled. '*Gotta talk!*'

Another pause, and then the rock-falls changed character as Harp started down a hundred yards ahead.

Stillwell sank to his back in the mud. He still didn't have his wind, he was covered with dirt and tangled vines, he had lost his hat and he had a roaring, ravening thirst. Over him stood Jersey Jack, still swaying, punchy with fatigue, refusing, old fighter that he was, to go down. His face was made up of two eyeholes in a layer of red ooze.

Out of the heavy brush at the left staggered Marshall. His shirt was torn off and his torso covered with whip-like welts. His pants were in tatters as if someone had slit them with razors. He weaved and stumbled and dropped beside Stillwell, his lungs going like a smith's bellows.

No one spoke. It was enough trouble breathing.

In another few moments, Harp appeared out of the vegetation to the right. He had been ahead, all right, and except for a coating of rock-dust and the knee out of his pants, looked in good shape. Stillwell wondered distantly why the top killers always seemed to maintain their composure and appearance better than the ordinary scuds.

Harp walked in, sank to a sitting position, legs crossed Indian-fashion. Beneath the coating of red chalk on his face, he was pale. This gave Stillwell some distant satisfaction.

'Now what?' Harp panted.

'It's getting up toward noon,' Stillwell said thickly. 'We've chased the little so and so all over the landscape. If we mess around any longer, we won't have time to get to town for the bank.'

Harp shook his head. 'He's got to be just ahead.'

'We thought that an hour ago,' Stillwell reminded him.

Marshall panted, 'I thought I heard him a while ago, just before you yelled. There was this mushy sound.'

'That was Jack falling in a mudhole.'

Marshall frowned, puzzled. 'It sounded ahead.'

'This whole area,' Stillwell pointed out wearily, 'is a puzzle. We guessed a while ago when we took the deeper fork. That kid might not even *be* ahead of us; he might be in that other fork—might be five miles from here right now.'

No one replied. Stillwell let them mull it a while. He was so tired, silence felt like a positive pleasure.

It was an odd thing. He hadn't wanted the kid killed. He had taken a mighty big chance, letting the runt have a chance at freedom that way. And yet, once the kid had dived over the lip of the gully and vanished, tumbling, into the heavy vegetation, Stillwell had really gotten caught up in the chase. It was as if he had given the kid his chance, and now by God he was going to take it back if he possibly could.

So they had chased hard and fast, and even cleverly, splitting up, making a wall, catching a sound to give them sense of direction, and running full-out through cover and over terrain that ordinarily would have killed a man in ten minutes.

But hell, the kid was no dummy after all. He had tricked them first by clinging to a side wall someplace and letting them go *right by him*. Then he had out-smarted them by taking the shallower fork. And now they hadn't seen him for an hour, and he was flat *gone*. Escaped.

Stillwell didn't know if he was glad or not. He did know he felt like a fool, and frustrated.

'We can't,' Harp said finally, 'just let him go.'

'He's already gone,' Stillwell said. 'We got no say in the matter.'

'He'll warn Bricker.'

'He's on foot. He's got no chance of getting there before two o'clock.'

Marshall consulted his watch. 'I dunno if *we* got a chance of getting there by two, now.'

'We can,' Stillwell said. 'Barely.'

'How?'

'We can climb out of this gully and go straight cross-country, back to camp. Ride hard. We can make it by two.'

'I,' Harp growled, 'don't like to let the kid go.'

'We can chase him,' Marshall suggested sarcastically, 'and let the bank job go.'

Harp put his hand on his gun. 'Don't get smart with me, buster!'

'Calm down,' Stillwell ordered sharply.

Jersey Jack spoke thoughtfully. 'I wanna do duh bank,' he grunted. 'I wanna blow id ub.'

Stillwell nodded. 'I say we climb out of here and get cracking.'

'I agree,' Marshall said wearily.

Harp glared at them. 'All right,' he said at last.

Stillwell looked around. He could make out sunlight up the right bank. 'We'll go up here,' he said.

They agreed with their silence. He got creakily to his feet. *God*, he was tired! He led the way.

It took fifteen minutes, and one nasty fall, but they climbed out. Up on the flat grass again, they started back for camp. The sun beat on them and the mud and sweat and blood and dirt all mixed together in fresh oozy body fluids and their own stink rose up around them like a cloud, drawing swarms of flies. They cursed and swatted as they stumbled along.

The kid might have gotten away, Stillwell thought, but they could still make it to the bank. It would be close, they wouldn't be at their best, but it was all going to work out. They could push themselves. All that money was worth it. Barring any more messes, they would be there.

Despite everything, the thought buoyed him. He began almost to feel human again. They were still the Stillwell Mob, he reminded himself, and they had their reputation to uphold. By two o'clock they would be there. He intended to see to it.

Chapter Twelve

The clock in front of the bank struck noon.

Adam Bricker walked towards the big brick building, dust from a passing wagon sifting down on him and sticking in his sweat.

The street was crowded now, almost jammed here and there with the farm wagons and drover supply trucks. Horsemen moved everywhere, and families with women and children jammed the board sidewalks as the week's shopping trip became the week's top social event. Hopewell might doze during the week, but on Saturdays it was nearly a city. This was the peak time.

The heat heightened Bricker's sense of foreboding. A veteran of this kind of country might make it for days without water or food. But little Clovis was no veteran.

There was still no word from the searchers, which meant they had found nothing. Bricker's skin crawled with mounting desperation. Billy Dean and the eight men helping him with the search would straggle in this afternoon; exhaustion would force them in. Bricker had to have another search party ready to go out.

Wearily he turned into the telegraph office. The old man behind the counter squinted at him from the brow of a green eyeshade.

'Lookin' for somethin' from San Francisco, Sheriff?' he guessed.

'Yes,' Bricker said.

'Got nothin', Sheriff. Sorry.'

Bricker turned and went back outside. He really hadn't expected anything. Walking down the scantily shaded sidewalk, he ran into Adele and Bobby, coming the other way.

'We've been looking for you,' Adele said, frowning.

'More trouble?'

Bricker grunted.

'No more,' Bobby said solemnly. 'But we want to help you about Clovis.'

Bricker leaned against the wall and built a smoke. 'How?'

'Have you thought of going into some of the saloons and telling them about Clovis and everything, and asking just *anybody* to help?'

'I have,' Bricker said. 'I did that last night and I've just been to two more saloons in the last few minutes.'

Bobby looked hopeful. 'How many men do you have?'

'None.'

'What,' Adele asked, 'if *we* asked them?'

'Right,' Bobby chimed in, liking the idea. 'They might have more sympathy, you know?'

'I know,' Bricker sighed. He added, 'It won't work.'

'Why not?' Adele demanded.

'Because!' Bricker began, but then swallowed his bitterness. 'Because they won't, that's all.' There was no need, he thought, looking at these two bright, worried kids, to dump any of his bitterness on them.

To ease their disappointment, he asked, 'Where's Doreen? And Ellen?'

'At home,' Adele said. 'Doreen is watching Ellen.'

'You better get back. We might stand to lose another kid this way.'

'No,' Adele said. '*I'm* going to help you find volunteers.'

'I just told you—!'

'If you won't let me help you ask, I'll help anyway,' Adele said.

'That's right,' Bobby added grimly. '*He's our brother.*'

The hot retort died on Bricker's tongue. He looked at them again. They were right. And they *had* a right. And just up the street was Bagwell's.

'All right,' he said. 'Come on.'

He led the way, and Adele and Bobby followed. It was a chance . . . the only one left to him.

The swinging doors of Bagwell's flapped loudly as he strode inside. There was a good crowd, and, as usual on Saturday afternoon, townspeople and drovers mixed. Those nearest the door took one look at his face and stilled instantly, and as he walked toward the bar to make his announcement, a hush fell.

Clovis lay flat on his belly and lapped up the icy water from the tiny spring. Surrounded by dense underbrush and stickers, he felt like a burrowing animal in its maze, like a mole or maybe a rabbit. His wild flight had torn most of his clothes off, and he felt the warm, wet earth against bare skin. The cold spring water hurt his gut, but he needed it badly.

They were not chasing him any more. He knew that. Either they had given up or he had fooled them when he went up the gully wall and down the draw and through the ditch and then into this side canyon. He had put a lot of miles between the place of his dive and this little spring. He hadn't heard any sign of pursuit at all for more than an hour. So he had shaken them.

That left only a few problems.

For one thing, he was on the ragged edge of sheer exhaustion. His legs shook every time he tried to stand on them. He had badly twisted his right ankle, too, falling down a cliff, and had lost a couple of fingernails trying to catch himself on the face of sheer rock. His bloody hands hurt a lot. Also, he was hungry and weak.

And he had absolutely no idea where he was anyhow. He was lost. Boy, he had really messed it up.

Lying under some stickers, Clovis noticed—again— that they bore some kind of fruit. He had noticed that earlier, and his naked carcass bore the purply stains of them mixed with his own blood from the thorns. The fruit looked like berries, and they smelled good. Now Clovis had read just enough dime novels to know a lot of good-looking fruits that grew wild would make a man go haywire, or even die. But he had also read about mountain men who subsisted on wild berries. He didn't know which way his particular brand of luck might be running, toward death or subsistence.

He reached up, without having to change basic position, and pulled down one of the berries. He tasted it.

It was warm and fairly sweet and tasted like wild raspberry.

He swallowed it and he didn't start dying right away, so he ate some more. Then, the first few down, he figured they would already have killed him if they were going to, so he ate a lot more. He actually liked them, and wolfed them in.

They made him thirsty, so he drank again, and, after a while, rolled over onto his back again.

'The boy has been gone almost twenty-four hours,' Bricker told them, standing on the bar and looking down at the sea of upturned faces. 'He doesn't know how to find food or water. Someone might have grabbed him, or he might have fallen into something and broken a leg. It's a desperate situation. I need volunteers to help look for him.'

The men stared up at him, saying nothing. A few averted their faces.

Bricker held his temper. 'He might be dying out there right now. I asked some of you last night, and you were busy. Maybe you're not too busy now. The nine men I've got out now will be coming back for a few hours' rest. I need at least a dozen fresh men to keep the search going. Now who's going to volunteer?'

No one spoke. A murmur of voices spread across the room. Men shuffled around, and the crowd around the bar began to break up on the edges.

'Anybody?' Bricker asked, fighting rage.

The mumbling grew louder, but no one spoke up.

At Bricker's feet, Bobby tugged his pant leg. 'Let us try.'

'All right, come on up,' Bricker said.

Bobby clambered up on the bar, and then, his face flushing, stooped to help Adele come up in a flurry of petticoats. The two of them stood beside Bricker. Voices in the room mumbled louder.

Bobby faced them, his earnest young face working. 'Clovis is the name of the boy that's missing,' he said, and the voices stilled. Bobby went on, 'He's my little brother. He's not too smart . . . I mean, he's *smart*, all right, but he doesn't know about taking good care of himself. Heckfire, one time on the train coming out here, Clovis got off for a drink of water and almost got back on the wrong train. So you can see he wouldn't be much 'count taking care of himself out in the country with snakes and everything.'

Bobby paused. The place had gotten very quiet. 'He's a pretty good little brother, though,' Bobby resumed. 'He does nice stuff, like he takes care of his younger sisters, he doesn't hurt anybody, he likes people. And he's real young, you know? And he doesn't deserve to die, even if he does do dumb stuff sometimes. So I'm asking you. I'm Bobby Wintle, some of you know my dad, I'm asking you to please help. Now I think my sister wants to ask you, too.'

Bobby paused and turned to Adele. She faced the crowd with a stricken pallor, except for bright pink spots of suffused excitement on her cheeks. She looked very, very young, and extremely beautiful and frightened.

'Clovis needs help,' she said, and broke down and began crying.

The men in the saloon stood there, and the soft, sweet,

ugly sounds of Adele's crying kept on. She turned to Bricker. 'I'm sorry—' Then she leaned against her brother, and Bobby helped her down off the bar.

Bricker himself was touched. It was genuine. He stood there a minute or two, and the men's voices rose up in increasing volume as they rattled to one another about the situation.

'All right,' Bricker said loudly. 'Who's going to volunteer?'

The men stared up at him: Quint the baker, Rife, Simkins, Sturgis, many familiar faces . . . middle-aged men and younger men, married and single, roughly weather-beaten and pallid from working in stores.

'Who?' Bricker repeated.

Nobody spoke. A couple of men in front turned their back, shame-faced but steadfast in their refusal. Somebody toward the back started a conversation about something else, and then in an ocean-like woosh there were a dozen idle conversations.

They were pretending it hadn't happened.

'I don't *understand*!' Adele said, her face tear-streaked.

'Bobby, take her outside,' Bricker suggested. 'I'll be right out.'

As Bobby led Adele through the ragged group toward the door, Bricker felt a tap on his back. He turned to see U. S. Bagwell, wearing his work apron.

'I'm going,' Bagwell said angrily.

'I told you last night,' Bricker said. 'You can't. These people will tear your saloon up while you're gone.'

'Damn the saloon, then. I'm going.'

Bricker looked at his friend.

'All right,' Bricker said, and went to the door.

Outside, Adele and Bobby stood in the blistering heat.

'I know one thing,' Bobby shot back. 'I'm going out in the second search group!'

Bricker made an instantaneous decision. 'All right, Bobby. Fine.'

'And I am too,' Adele said.

'No, you're not. You're staying here. You're watching after the others.'

'But I want—'

'You don't always do what you want,' Bricker said. 'You do what you have to, sometimes, because that's the way things are.'

The two of them looked at him.

'Savvy?' Bricker asked.

'Yes,' Adele said, faltering.

'I guess so,' Bobby said, unconvinced and glowering.

'Okay,' Bricker grunted. 'Adele, you get back home. Take care of the other kids. Bobby, go to the livery, pick you out a horse. I've got some calls to make.'

'Calls?' Bobby echoed.

'To get us our volunteers,' Bricker said.

'But nobody will—'

'There's more than one way,' Bricker quoted, 'to skin a cat.'

Chapter Thirteen

Five minutes before two, and Hopewell was sliding into the hot Saturday afternoon doldrums.

Standing in the scant shade of the hardware store awning, Preacher Addison looked the situation over and found it to his liking. Only two big wagons remained on the street in the blocks on either side of the bank, one parked in at an angle for loading at Kirk's Feed Store, the other up against the sidewalk with the team unhooked and taken off to a livery. A handful of people walked around the streets. A number of horses remained queued up outside saloons, but even the horse population seemed down since the sheriff had taken a large group of men over toward the jail for a conflab.

That had shaken Addison badly when he first spotted it, but a quick check had informed him the true situation. So a kid was missing and Bricker was organizing a search party. Addison smiled to himself. That was even better than apple dumplings. Everything was going to go smooth as gravy.

It was time.

Addison stepped out of the shade and started up the

sidewalk the half block toward the bank. Passing two elderly women, he smiled and touched the brim of his hat in a courtly gesture. They smiled warmly.

As Addison moved nearer the bank, he saw Tommy Delbert stroll around the far corner and walk jauntily into the building, hands jammed in his pockets. Then, almost simultaneously, he spotted Jeff Simms walking up from the opposite end of the block, on the far side of the street. Fred Green was leaning out front of the brick structure, making a smoke. As Addison neared the building next to the bank, he spotted Donnie Hawkins coming out of the saloon across the way.

Addison hummed to himself as he walked on to the bank corner, gave the lounging Green the slightest eye-flash, and went inside.

The clock up overhead chimed once. Then it chimed again.

The old man who served as uniformed guard was at the door, but Addison gave him an apologetic smile and the old man stepped back to let him in. It was dim inside, but there were several other customers, which screwed things up for the old man who couldn't lock the door on the stroke of two as he otherwise might. Addison walked to a deposit counter and frowned at the card giving instructions on how to make a deposit.

The card might as well have been written in Greek. For Addison wasn't reading it at all. He was seeing a dozen other things at once: the old lady at the pay-out wicket, the schoolteacher at the draft-writing counter, the merchant standing at the far end, talking with the man who evidently was the banker, and an elderly codger in white suit with spats and a hat, strolling around the middle of the lobby, gawking and swinging a pearl-headed cane.

Addison was also seeing that the old guard's was the only gun in sight, and the bank vault door stood partly open, and reflected sunlight shafted in from somewhere and made it glow like the gold it contained. Addison's mouth had begun to go dry with tension, but mentally he could feel it watering for all that loot.

It was now a minute after two.

Addison was still at the counter. Green, of course, was outside where he would stay as lookout. Tommy Delbert was in: down at the end near the banker and the merchant. Jeff Simms was in, standing near the door and making some kind of conversation with the bald old guard. And Donnie Hawkins was in; he was near the windows.

The old lady at the wicket finished her business and shuffled to the door, and out. The schoolteacher put his papers away and left behind her. The merchant took out his watch, glanced at it, snapped it closed, and said something to the banker. The banker said something to the teller and that young man closed his wicket, went around the end of the counter, and lowered a shade. He started for the second shade, encountering Donnie Hawkins on the way.

'I'm sorry, sir.' The teller smiled. 'We're closing.'

Hawkins smiled back, took out his Colt, and stuck it in the youth's belly. 'That's okay, pardner. This is a holdup.'

At the door, the old guard yelped and Jeff Simms deftly clipped him alongside the head with the barrel of his gun. By this time the banker and the man in white saw what was going on, but Tommy Delbert had them covered. Addison went over the counter, glanced in the back office, spotted no one, and ran back into the front.

'Jeff,' he snapped, 'lock that front door and get the other shades. You men over there, lay down on the floor, face down. Donnie, if they mess around, club 'em. Tommy, get in that vault and start sacking the money.'

Tommy went around the corner of the counter on the double and swung the bank vault door wide. It whispered on ball bearings, a lovely, rich sound.

The old codger in the white outfit snorted at Addison, 'I say, sir, have this person cease and desist! The idea of lying upon the floor of a public building is repugnant to me, to say the least. And may I point out, you dastardly cur, that you are dealing with Colonel T. T. Clydesdale of the—'

'Donnie,' Addison said, 'hit him.'

'All right!' the colonel yelped, going to the floor with shocking agility. 'All right—under protest of the sternest sort, I assure you!'

From the vault came Tommy Delbert's hushed voice. 'Preach, there's gold in here like you wouldn't *believe*!'

Addison grinned at Hawkins, standing over the prone prisoners, and Jeff, guarding the front door.

At that moment, with a slight, funny, hissing implosion, the back door of the building came off its hinges.

'Well,' Helen Jefferson sighed, 'I just think you're an awful fool.'

'Maybe,' Bricker admitted, facing her across his desk. 'But Billy ought to be back any minute, and I told these boys to be ready to go by five. Billy and the others can lead them. They'll meet in the park and go from there, and by midnight I'll bet you we have Clovis safe.'

'Oh, I know it'll work,' Helen groaned. 'And it's a good thing.'

'Then what's the big complaint?'

'You have to run for re-election in this town, and soon!'

'The kid has to be found.'

Helen grimaced. 'I know what you did, Adam Bricker! It's not a secret even now! You went to Criswell the barber, and Rife and Baker and I don't know how many more, and *threatened* them into serving on this second search party that goes out at five o'clock!'

Bricker grinned. 'I didn't threaten anybody.'

'Oh, of course not! You just told Criswell that if he didn't volunteer, you couldn't guarantee that you'd have any free time to check his shop in the night!'

'I got thirteen volunteers, didn't I?'

'They'll remember. They'll vote against you.'

'It's a good town,' Bricker grunted. 'With good people. But sometimes I think it'd take a real disaster to get 'em motivated. I just helped them along, that's all.'

Helen looked shocked. 'You act like you'd *like* a disaster!'

'Nope. I've got quite enough disasters already.'

'Did anyone,' Helen asked, 'ever tell you you're too proud?'

'Often.'

'You're a proud and stubborn man.'

'Right.'

She smiled wanly. 'You know you bring trouble on yourself sometimes.'

'I do all right,' Bricker bluffed.

'Don't you ever get . . . lonely?' she asked dubiously.

Bricker watched her and wondered how to reply. He made up his mind. 'All people get lonely. It's part of living. It's like pain. People come in and complain they've got a gut ache, or their bunions hurt. I suppose I'm supposed to feel sorry for them. I just cluck, usually. But they ought to know pain is normal. It's living.'

Helen looked at him a long time. 'You're a very difficult person to know,' she said finally.

'You know me.'

She shook her head. 'I don't know if I do or not.'

Bricker hesitated, sensing that it was a very unusual and sensitive moment. A little while ago she had been mad as a wet hen with him about Adele. Now she was worried about him. He felt that she was open to him right now—and he to her—in a way they hadn't experienced before. Bricker had known the feeling only with one other person.

She was too damned lovely, Bricker thought. She was handsome and strong and beautiful, and he ached for her. He didn't know how to put it, but the moment might not come again.

'So you're worried about me,' he grunted.

'Yes,' she smiled quietly.

'Well, that's okay. I worry about you sometimes, too.'

'Do you?'

Bricker plunged in, fumbling. 'Helen, listen. I don't talk good. But we'll find Clovis. I'll find John Wintle, too, and get this thing with the kids straightened out. With any luck, I can round these gangs up between now and election, or at least get a good start. With a little more luck, I can get re-elected. That'll make things more secure. A lawman doesn't make a lot of money and it's a hell of a thing to ask, but—'

'Boy, howdy!' a voice groaned from the doorway, and Billy Dean reeled into the office.

Startled, Helen turned just as Bricker broke off in mid-sentence. Billy Dean was sweaty and coated with dust. His eyes were red-rimmed and he looked utterly beat.

'We didn't find a trace,' he announced, flopping into a chair. 'I told the boys to go on home and get a few hours' shuteye, and we'd get on it again about five or six. Is that okay, boss?'

Bricker looked at Helen, then nodded. He felt a sharp sense of loss. The moment between them had suddenly vanished.

Startled half out of his wits, Preacher Addison spun toward the dirty implosion at the back door. It had been a hinge job: very quiet, not even much smoke. A dim figure charged through the swirling cloud, with another man—then another and still another—right behind him. A piece of the plaster ceiling fell down, making a new puffy cloud.

The first man in was dark, bearded, rough-clothed, and vaguely familiar. He had his gun in his hand. So did the others.

'Everybody freeze!' he bellowed. 'This is a holdup!'

'The hell you say!' Addison yelled back, too stunned to use the gun in his own hand.

'Who are you?' The newcomer demanded, eyes glinting.

One of his men cried, 'Hey, boss, what the—?'

Preacher Addison began to understand what had happened, and it blew his mind. He stared over his gun barrel at the other gang leader, at the thin young killer behind him, at the third man, who carried a shotgun, and at the fourth, a hulking giant with a smashed face and a small sack over his shoulder. At the same time, with his peripheral vision, Addison had his own men sighted: Tommy Delbert crouched by the door of the vault, Donnie Hawkins standing with gun in hand beside the prone prisoners toward the far end of the room, Jeff Simms by the windows. Nobody was moving or saying anything at all, and it was silent as a few last chunks of ceiling fell.

'I said,' the bearded man snapped, 'who are you?'

'Who the hell are *you*?' Addison countered.

'We're the Stillwell Mob, and we're robbing this bank.'

'Yeah?' Preacher Addison returned. 'Well, we're the Hole in the Wall Gang, and we got here first!'

Fred Stillwell—it had to be he—jerked like a man shot in the back. His face twitched as he digested the information. His hand with the gun lowered involuntarily to his side.

'Oh,' he said.

'So,' Addison blustered, 'you guys better just turn around and get out of here. We're right in the middle of this thing and we don't have a lot of time and you're in the way.'

'We're not going anywhere.' Stillwell shot back, his gun coming up again. 'We came to rob this here bank and we intend to do it.'

Behind Stillwell, the cold-eyed young gunman murmured, 'I've got the one near the door, boss.'

'Shut up,' Stillwell ordered nervously.

The big man with the smashed face uncoiled the sack from his shoulder and sat it down on the floor with a thump. Stillwell blanched. 'Jack, watch that sack! That dynamite is sweating! You want to blow up the whole place? One bad bump, and—'

'Hugh,' the hulk grunted. 'Boom! Huh huh huh.'

Preacher Addison felt a distinct chill. Nobody had made a serious move yet, but he knew—felt with the prickling on his scalp—that bullets might be flying thicker than bees in a hive just any second. The careless handling of the dynamite—it looked like a *hell* of a lot, too—added a dimension of terror that wasn't really necessary.

'You better get out,' he tried firmly.

'*You* better get out,' Stillwell countered angrily.

'We got here first!'

'We're the Stillwell Mob!'

'*We're* the Hole in the Wall Gang! Are you out of your mind? *Nobody* messes with the Hole in the Wall Gang!'

Stillwell sneered. 'Somebody just did, buster. Out!'

Preacher Addison took a long, slow breath. He had his gun on Stillwell's middle. Stillwell had *his* gun on Addison's middle. Neither of them really wanted to fire, because the other bullet probably would pass the first in mid-course, and people who got gut-shot seldom lived to brag about it.

'First shot,' Addison told Stillwell, 'and the law comes down on all of us.'

'Then get out quiet,' Stillwell suggested.

'Man, you got some kind of nerve! We got here first, and—'

'Are you going to do what I say or not?'

At that moment, Jeff Simms rattled the blind at the window. 'Boss!'

Addison didn't turn. He kept his attention riveted on his rival. 'Hold it, Jeff.'

'No, listen!' Simms hissed. 'There's two old coots out on the steps, giving Fred a bad time! They've got badges on!'

'Bricker?' Addison asked, a chill going through him.

'No, they're *old*. They got these old rusty badges, and Fred's shoving them back down the steps, and—oh-oh!'

'What?' Stillwell barked.

'What?' Addison repeated.

'The one old guy just kicked Fred in the—he doubled him over and now—'

Window glass shattered. The front door burst open. In rushed two of the crummiest, randiest, dirtiest old men Preacher Addison had ever beheld. They had guns in hand—old guns, rusty and everything else, but probably still lethal enough—and badges glowed red with more rust on their underwear shirts.

'All right!' the first old man snarled toothlessly. 'Everybody stand fast! We're robbin' this here bank and it's only fair to warn you, we're the Hash Knife!'

'Oh, good God,' Addison groaned.

'This is ridiculous!' Stillwell grunted.

Near the vault, Tommy Delbert raised his gun and snapped a shot at one of the old men. Glass shattered. The old man yelled an obscenity and fired back. The old gun shot a cloud of black powder and a slug whined past Preacher Addison's ear. He went for the deck, and all at the same time Stillwell started shooting, his men started shooting, the shotgun went off, Jeff and Donnie dived for cover and opened up, the old men scattered in both directions, Fred came staggering in through the door, one hand to his groin, another piece of the ceiling fell, bullets began bouncing wickedly in all directions, somebody went out a window head-first, more glass shattered, a desk seemed to blow up under the impact of a shotgun blast, somebody screamed in pain, the whole room was filled with dense powder smoke, and men were running and jumping and diving and firing all over the place, and Preacher Addison rolled for the wall, wishing he could shoot somebody, out of sheer frustration if for no other reason, but his goddam gun had jammed, the hammer was stuck somehow. He lay behind an overturned desk against the wall, fighting with his stuck gun hammer, cursing monotonously under his breath, and bullets splattered into the plaster over his head, showering him with prickly white dust.

In his office, Bricker was explaining his plan for the search to Billy Dean, who smiled dutifully and tried valiantly to stay awake. The distant gunfire seemed to explode all at once, and Bricker was on his feet and in the street, running, before Dean had even reacted.

Gun in hand, Bricker ran toward the bank corner. Other men were running too, in all directions. He spotted a half-dozen townspeople; merchants, clustered on the corner a block from the bank. He could see smoke coming from the bank windows.

Chapter Fourteen

Flat on the floor behind the table, Preacher Addison finally got his gun hammer unjammed. The spring wasn't broken and it seemed all right. A window exploded in bright shards of glass just to his left, and somebody yelled hoarsely. The din was making his hearing shut off, the bank was so filled with smoke he couldn't see as far as the vault, but somebody was firing over there because the orange muzzle-flashes cut the smoke.

Peering around the end of the table, Addison took one despairing look-see, then jerked his head back just as a slug smashed into the plaster where his face had been.

Jeff Simms had bought it, or was at best knocked out, stretched face-down on the floor near the counter. The inside of the room was a shambles, and men were moving around for better cover or firing lines. It was getting worse.

Addison watched one of the old men scuttle wildly across the open floor toward the vault. Addison considered shooting him and then just decided against it. The old man scuttered out of view.

Addison decided he couldn't just lie there. He would get shot anyway. He wondered fleetingly whether he should fight or try the other idea forming in his mind. He made up his mind so quickly that he had jumped to his feet and was in violent motion across the room before he even reasoned it out.

Bullets sang around him and somebody yelled hoarsely. He didn't get hit, somehow. Through the smoke he saw the counter and wickets ahead. He left his feet and sailed over them, head-first.

Sure enough, Stillwell hadn't moved much in the seconds since the hell all broke loose. He was crouched there behind the counter, and his eyeballs looked big as Addison flew over the counter and came down wide-armed, crashing on top of him with sickening impact. They hit together and rolled back against the heavy door of the vault, and Stillwell screamed and tried to bring his Colt around, but Addison came out on top and jammed his own revolver barrel hard up under Stillwell's chin.

Stillwell's eyes really bugged now, but he froze.

Nobody else even knew it was happening. They were too busy blowing more chunks off the walls and furniture and each other.

'*Listen*, dammit!' Addison yelled in Stillwell's ear. 'We gotta stop!'

'How?' Stillwell croaked.

'We've drawn attention from the town. They'll have us surrounded in a minute. We gotta get together or we're *all* going to be killed!'

Stillwell's bugged eyes stared, watery, into Addison's.

The two men held for an instant, locked together, struggling, with Addison's gun in Stillwell's throat.

'Split the money?' Stillwell asked huskily.

'Listen, we're going to grab one bag and hightail. You can have anything you think you're man enough to haul outta here!'

Stillwell nodded. 'Lemme loose.'

Addison relaxed his grip.

Stillwell turned on his hip. *'Hold it, you guys!'* he bellowed.

The shooting went right on, and another big chunk of ceiling came down.

'Hold it, HOLD IT!' Stillwell screamed, waving his arms.

Some of the shooting tapered off, and then for a magical instant it got still, as if everyone had paused to reload at once.

Addison bellowed, *'Truce! Everybody stop firing!'*

'What?' someone called from the front. Delbert, maybe. Well, it was a desperate gamble, but Preacher Addison boldly stood up.

'We're calling it off,' he grunted.

At that instant, the front windows of the bank became a hurricane as what seemed like an army's amount of bullets began hurtling through, bouncing off walls, singing in all directions. Addison hit the floor.

'They got us surrounded!' one of his men shrilled up front.

Addison stared at Stillwell. Stillwell stared at Addison. From out of the vault crawled one of the two old men, the one with no teeth. His hair, what there was of it, stood straight on end.

'I don't like this deal!' the old man said.

Addison and Stillwell said nothing. For once they were all in agreement.

Adam Bricker had run down the street, taken one look, and gotten part of the picture. He yelled at a man across the street to grab the reins of all the horses tied alongside the bank, and get them out of there. The man nodded and ran raggedly for the nearest hitching rack, but just about the time he got a handful of reins, the first citizens with—Bricker almost fell down with shock—guns in their hands ran out from a hardware across the street. The men went to their bellies and started firing blindly at the bank building. Windows blew inward and smoke billowed out and a slug hit one of the horses and it went down, screaming, and the other horses bolted in all directions. The only remaining wagon team in the block went berserk with the noise and excitement, and charged right down the middle of the street, almost dehorning half the scattered vigilantes, who broke in every direction. Somebody shot a window out on the wrong side of the street and a fistfight broke out, but more men were running to join. It looked like an army, and Bricker couldn't tell whether they were in full attack or all-out retreat. There wasn't any firing coming back from the bank. . . .

Billy Dean ran up, out of breath. 'They're robbing the bank, boss!'

'I got that impression.'

Men were dragging barrels and boxes out of stores, tables out of saloons, making barricades. A murderous, continuous hail of lead was banging into and against the bank. Pieces were being blown off the brick front. Two of the vigilantes were down, rolling in agony. Somebody wasn't shooting very straight.

Bricker made some decisions. 'Billy. Get over there and try to get them to stop shooting. There's going to be a damned massacre. Tell them you're in charge. Flash your badge. Slug somebody. I don't care how. *Get them stopped.*'

'But the bank's being robbed!' Billy protested.

'I *know* that. Do what you're told!'

His deputy ran toward the skirmish line of butchers, bakers, and candlestick-makers.

Bricker continued to crouch behind the edge of the building. He didn't know what had happened inside the bank, but obviously the whole thing had gone decidedly sour for the would-be robbers. They might be smart enough to know it, too. They had two chances to escape, now: little and none. Bricker by now was worried more about the outlaws being slaughtered than he was about escape. Maybe the men inside were smart enough to see that too.

The front of the bank seemed suddenly to sag and buckle inward. The windowframes vanished and the roof raised about a foot, then came back right in place with such quickness that Bricker wondered if he had seen it. Then the front door blew off in a million pieces and a huge black cloud billowed out, and the thunderclap of the explosion blasted Bricker back against the wall. Planks flew, shingles sailed, and bricks showered into the street.

Bricker knew he had not time to try to figure it out. This was his chance.

Although a few hysterical merchants were firing into the billowing cloud and showering chunks of building, Bricker heaved himself away from the protective corner of his building and ran.

He charged into the street, ignoring the townsmen's bullets which hummed around him, and headed for the shattered front door of the bank at a dead run.

Bricker reached the front area of the bank, ran through broken glass, jumped a big chunk of oak door-frame, and vaulted the steps covered with rubble of all kinds. He ploughed into the dense, swirling smoke and plaster dust choking the interior of the building.

Most of the ceiling was down. Timbers lay at crazy angles. He saw two men sprawled unconscious on the floor to the right, another sitting dazed against a broken bench to the left, another face-down on the floor near his feet. He spotted several men's figures staggering, dazed, in the smoke.

'All right!' he yelled. 'I'm the sheriff! Give it up right now or you're dead, all of you!'

A voice croaked through the smoke, 'Give it up, boys! He's right, we got no chance now.'

With the words, a man staggered out of the wreckage, hands up.

Bricker almost dropped his gun with shock. It was Fred Stillwell. Covered with plaster dust and blood, he was still recognizable. His eyes were glassy with shock. 'I'm givin' up, Bricker, damn your ass.'

Bricker recovered. He waggled his gun. 'Line up.'

Another figure staggered forward, and then more men appeared, hands over their heads.

Behind Bricker, somebody charged through the

rubble. Billy Dean appeared beside him, wild-eyed, gun ready.

'We got them.' Bricker snapped. 'Tell the men outside. Have them make a circle. *No shooting*. Tell them.'

For once, Dean understood. He whirled and ran out, and Bricker could hear him yelling instructions. Men began to whoop.

Bricker didn't have time to pay attention to any of that, however. He was staring at one of his other prisoners, a lank man who appeared to have had his shirt and most of his pants blown clean off by the explosion.

'Aren't you Preacher Addison?' Bricker gasped.

'If a slug hadn't hit these idiots' dynamite, we'd of made it yet,' Addison snarled.

Bricker managed to keep his face on straight. Inwardly he was reeling. Stillwell: the Stillwell Mob. Addison: the Hole in the Wall Gang. *Had they been teamed up?*

No time to think it out.

'Pick up the ones that can't walk,' Bricker ordered, 'and file out of here past me. Now listen: I've got a small army of trigger-happy people out there. Don't make any funny moves or I can't be responsible.'

Preacher Addison stumbled over and helped a man, groaning, to his feet. Addison kept him up and looked wearily back at Bricker. 'We're not doing anything funny. Just keep 'em off our backs.'

Bricker nodded and backed nearer the door. 'Billy!'

Dean was nearby. 'Yeah!' he sang out.

'They're coming out. They've surrendered. Got that? Does everybody understand that?'

There was some ragged, rowdy cheering out in the street.

'Okay,' Bricker told Stillwell. 'Out.'

Stillwell nodded, beat. He stumbled toward the door, followed by a big, fat-faced man supporting a slender youth, and then another man with face covered by blood.

'Is this all your people?' Bricker asked.

'It's all of them,' Stillwell grated.

Bricker turned to Addison. The gang leader supported one man, another of his group had a companion on his back. A tall, gangling boy stumbled along behind.

'All of yours?' Bricker asked.

'Yeah,' Addison grunted disgustedly.

Bricker stood in the door and they all filed out into the sunshine. The townspeople ringing the area whooped and hollered with glee.

Bricker glanced around the interior of the bank. It looked pretty well wrecked. The smoke was still dense, but he knew he had everyone out because neither gang leader had any reason to lie. Through the smoke and settling dust, past a slanted, wrecked roof timber, glowed the door of the vault.

It was incredible. But they hadn't made it. The bank was safe. Wrecked, maybe. But intact with its money.

Chapter Fifteen

Theodore was having a coughing fit inside the bank vault. Amos, crouched under the front window, covertly watched the mob of citizens and the sheriff and the prisoners herd down the street in the direction of the jail. It got quiet outside, and inside, too, except for the occasional sifting of dust from the shattered roof and Theodore's hacking cough.

'Quit the coughing,' Amos muttered, 'or they'll hear you!'

'Can't help it,' Theodore choked. 'This here thing's full of dust.'

'Then get out of there!'

'You think I'm crazy? It's full of money, too.'

It was almost unbelievable, but the sheriff had missed them in the confusion and smoke, Amos thought. Now the bank was empty except for them, and the street lay deserted too. They were in free, overlooked.

Left in the shattered bank with all that gold—and their horses still hidden out back in the alley.

Hardly able to believe their good luck, Amos limped around the remains of the bank counters and to the door of the vault. Inside, Theodore was on his hands and knees, hacking like his lungs would come up any second, scooping big gold coins into a sack with both hands. He was covered with chalky dust and looked like a spastic ghost.

'C'mon, Amos,' he managed between coughs. 'Help me get this stuff in sacks.'

'They already had plenty sacked up,' Amos pointed out, nudging a big bag of five and ten-dollar coins with the torn toe of his boot. 'We don't haf to sack any more.'

'Like hell we don't,' Theodore choked, still shovelling with both hands. 'They messed up. They forgot us. They forgot the old Hash Knife, boy, and we're gonna clean 'em out.'

'One of these bags weighs more'n a hunnert pounds, Theodore. We can't carry but a couple.'

'I can carry more'n that,' Theodore rasped. 'I ain't as old as I look, buster.'

Amos began to feel nervous. He glanced towards the front door again to reassure himself. The street lay deserted and silent. He turned back. 'Look, Theodore. One sack apiece and we're on easy street.'

'You take one if you want,' Theodore gasped, getting his second big canvas sack filled to the brim. '*I'm* takin' two.'

'All right,' Amos fretted. 'Take two if you want. Only let's git outta here before somebody comes back.'

Theodore got painfully to his feet. He looked around. His face slit in a ghastly, dusty, toothless grin. He began shuffling around, dancing. 'Oh, they forgot the old Hash Knife, hee-hee, they forgot the old Hash Knife—'

'Get 'em and let's go,' Amos muttered, hefting his

canvas sack. Ooóf! It weighed a ton. He staggered, getting it over his shoulder.

'Forgot the ole Hash Knife,' Theodore hummed. 'Forgot the ole Hash Knife, hee-hee.' He hefted his first sack. His eyes bulged and he weaved horribly. He got it up on his shoulder and then slung over his back. Sweat popped out of his forehead, coming through the chalky dust like flour water.

'Be satisfied with one,' Amos advised.

'Two,' Theodore grunted, reaching for the second.

Amos watched him knot the mouth of the overfilled sack and grab a good hold. Then Theodore planted his flat feet and lifted.

The sack didn't budge.

'*Uunh*,' Theodore said.

'Come on,' Amos fretted. 'Hurry up, hurry up.'

Theodore was frozen, bent over his second precious sack.

'Come *on*,' Amos urged, getting more nervous by the moment.

'Amos?' Theodore said, strangled.

'What? What?'

'I just ruptured myself.'

Out in the street in front of the jail, a dozen townsmen were tearing into the dirt street like madmen. Picks, shovels, and mattocks threw dirt all over the place. An even larger group stood around, brandishing their shotguns and whisky bottles, yelling congratulations at one another.

Adam Bricker, on the steps of the jail, stood with Jarvis Fody, U. S. Bagwell, Colonel T. T. Clydesdale, and Harold Enright. Inside the jail, Billy Dean was watching the prisoners, temporarily jammed into the small cells like sardines. The doc was on his way to handle the wounded.

'It was a deplorable moment,' the colonel intoned, swinging his white cane. 'Unless I took drastic and immediate action, I could see that the situation would get out of hand. Therefore, quick as a flash, I leaped through the window, at great personal risk, in order to alert the populace.'

'You tell 'em, Colonel,' one of the men in the crowd yelled gleefully.

Enright frowned over his notes. 'It's hard to believe. Two gangs trying to hit the bank at the same time.'

'It worked out,' Bricker said grimly still trying to convince himself it was all happening.

'And,' a man with a pick said, pausing to mop his forehead, 'we by gosh *helped*. All of us.'

'You better believe it!' another man with a shovel chortled. He held the shovel up to his shoulder like a gun. '*Wham! Bam!*'

Jarvis Fody patted Bricker on the back. 'I'd say civic pride has never been higher. And you rushing the bank. I saw that. It was heroic. Heroic.'

'I don't think so,' Bricker growled, 'I—'

'I agree,' Enright said briskly, making a note. 'Certainly there was *some* risk involved, and I congratulate you, Sheriff. However, there was great confusion. Anyone charged with your responsibility would have done the same.'

Bagwell looked hard at Enright. 'You bad-mouthing Adam again?'

'Oh, no,' Enright smiled. 'It's a remarkable feat. But let's keep things in perspective, shall we? If law enforcement had been up to snuff, would we have had two gangs to rob the bank in the first place?'

Mayor Steed waddled up through the crowd and swirling dust. 'I heard that, Harold.' The mayor's face was surprisingly hard. 'We saw something today. The town rose up and *did* something. You shut up that kind of talk.'

Enright paled visibly. 'I didn't mean to imply—'

'Good,' Steed grunted.

Smothering a smile, Bricker watched the men digging the prison pit. He felt awfully, awfully good.

Hopewell, perhaps, had been reborn.

Sobbing and spitting, Theodore sat on his horse in the alley, watching Amos stagger out with one of the overfilled sacks of gold.

'I hurt,' Theodore complained. 'I hurt real bad, Amos.'

'Shut up, shut up,' Amos groaned, dragging the overloaded sack. 'We still got this, you stupid ignoramus.'

'I dunno what I'm gonna do,' Theodore said, almost to the point of real tears.

'Since when did you think at all?'

'Half my gut come out down there. I can feel it. I really ruptured myself bad. I can't ride far.'

'Shut up and save your energy then!'

'Yeah, but you don't know how the pain is.'

At this instant, Amos tried to heft the bag onto his horse. The seam of the bag ripped and the whole contents—hundreds and hundreds of beautiful gold coins

—spilled down his front and all over the dirt floor of the alley.

'*Damn!*'

'You spilled it!' Theodore cried.

'You dumb toad-strangling greedy mothering old fool! I know what I done! Did you haf to fill it so full? That sack couldn't even *hold* all you shovelled in!'

'Git another, git another,' Theodore groaned, doubled over.

Amos waded through gold coins. He started inside. He spotted a movement out in the street—a skinny, muddy kid walking down the street. The kid looked completely beat, but Amos's movement caught his eye and he turned, stared at the blown-out front of the bank with wonderment, then obviously spotted Amos.

Tingling, Amos froze. Maybe he would walk on.

The kid stared.

Amos decided maybe he should act like he was cleaning up, so he began humming and kicking debris around. God, how he wished for a broom!

The kid started toward the bank, walking slowly, warily.

Amos cursed under his breath, picked up a broken ceiling rafter, and tossed it onto a larger pile of rubble.

From out back, Theodore groaned, 'What're you *doing*?'

'Hush, hush,' Amos hissed.

The kid picked his way through the shattered front of the building. He stared at Amos. Amos stared back. The kid was skinny, dirty, grey from fatigue. His clothes were torn and he was barefooted.

Amos decided to try desperate normalcy. 'Howdy' he grinned.

Clovis felt like he had been walking a hundred miles, which was only a fivefold exaggeration. His feet were blistered and the blisters had popped and oozed and the berries weren't sitting too well on his stomach and he was thirsty and worn out. But as he stood there in the rubble of the bank building, Clovis forgot about most of his own troubles.

The old man facing him looked like something left over from the climax of a dime novel. Soaked with sweat, covered with powdery plaster dust and red dirt, bearded and red-eyed, he would have looked spooky if he weren't so beat-up and bent-over. When the old man said, 'Howdy,' he grinned. But the grin was a death mask and the cheerful sound of his voice was more like the lid of a casket skreeking on bad hinges.

'Who are you?' Clovis asked, putting first things first.

The old man kept grinning desperately. 'Well, sonny, my name is John Smith. My, you're a nice-lookin' little feller, ain't you.' He tried to reach out to pat Clovis on the head. Or wring his neck.

Clovis moved back a few paces. 'What're you doing here, mister?'

'By golly,' the old man croaked, 'I'm cleaning up this mess!'

'What happened?'

'By golly, by gosh, sonny, you do ask good questions! You're a right smart little feller, you are!' The old man gave a funereal chuckle. 'Well, sonny, the sheriff ast me and my partner to clean up this mess. A gang tried to rob the bank, but the sheriff run 'em off.'

Clovis felt a burst of elation. 'He did? He ran 'em off?'

Clovis frowned at the wreckage. He was getting an awful lot of data very quickly. Too quickly. He was having trouble assembling it. It was clear that something had happened here, and the street was empty, which meant that something was over. He didn't understand, quite.

'Where's everybody else?' he asked.

The old man giggled horribly and tried to pat him again. Or wring his neck. 'Golly, that's a right smart question, little buddy! It sure is! Oh, well, everybody is over at the jail, see?'

'At the jail?' Clovis was uncertain.

'Yep! They caught these badmen, see, and they're over there. They're over there right now, and, boy, you ought to git over there and see the fun!'

'Fun?' Clovis echoed. Things didn't fit here. Lies were being told. He couldn't get things sorted out.

'Yeah!' the old man grinned. 'They're puttin' them badmen in jail, an' everybody's there. You ought to git over there right now, boy! You hurry, you might see some of it. My partner an' me, we'll stay here an' clean up, like the sheriff tole us ,to. See my badge?'

Clovis spotted the towsack full of gold on the floor, and some of the gold coins in the alley doorway. 'Where *is* your partner?' he asked.

'He's jus' outside, sonny.'

Clovis started for the back door.

'Hey, wait!'

Clovis stepped into the alley.

Two beat-up horses, the other old man bent double with pain in one saddle, the coins strewn all over the place.

That was when Clovis understood. He didn't understand the *how*, maybe, but he understood.

'You better git now, little bitty buddy,' the old man burbled.

The old man on the horse opened pained eyes. 'Who's *he*?'

'Jus' a kid,' the old man in the bank door muttered. 'C'mon now, sonny, you jus' skedaddle—'

'No,' Clovis said.

'Huh?' the old man gasped.

Clovis faced the two of them from the wall as the old man still on his feet sort of backed, lumbering, out into the alley and sidled toward his mounted partner. The old men looked scared—as scared as Clovis was.

'I think,' Clovis said, 'you two guys are trying to steal this money.'

'Aw!' the old man on foot grunted. 'Would we do that?'

It was perfectly clear, and to Clovis, a brilliant scheme leaped into mind. It was so simple and so easy, and he could make everything fine again.

All he had to do was yell his head off.

The two old coots were just staring at him. Scared to death, offering him no harm, trapped, done in and paralysed. They were at his mercy.

Clovis had never had anybody at his mercy before.

'Look, sonny, little buddy,' the one old man said eagerly. 'Tell you what, you nice kid. Jus' let us go—

okay? We'll jus' take a few of these here coins—jus' a handful, aw right?'

'No,' Clovis said, drawing breath again. 'You can't take anything.'

'Lookee here,' the old man afoot said eagerly. He reached down and scooped up a huge handful of heavy gold pieces. 'That much! That's all we'll take, see? An' lookee here, little boy buddy. You're smart. You know how hard it is to take money. You put a few in your pocket, see?' He held out a few coins, some of them twenties.

Clovis stared at the money, more than he had ever seen before. He was still thinking about being a hero and everything else and he was desperately mixed up.

'They'll never *miss 'em*!' the old man panted.

Clovis looked at him, trying to sort his thoughts out. Temptation knocked on his door and walked in and sat down on the sofa and felt pretty comfortable.

'An' here,' the old man added. He pulled a horribly rusted, beat-up old gun out of his holster. 'See this yere nice gun? It's yourn. It's got one bullet left in. See, this is what you do. You let us go, you let us take a few coins, see? Not much. Jus' a few. An' *you* take some. They won't never even miss 'em, see? An' then you give us five, ten minutes to git started, see? You're worried about gettin' caught. I know. Aw right, listen. You give us five, ten minutes to start, see? Then you shoot old Bess up in the air, see? An' you holler an' you scream an' you raise a commotion, see? An' when people come runnin', you say you run a couple of fellers off, young fellers, an' they headed north. *North.* Right?'

Clovis frowned, trying to keep up. Temptation had its feet up on the coffee table now.

'See?' the old man grinned. 'You let us go, you git the money, an' you're a hero, see? *You're a hero.* You run us off!'

'And you really head the other direction,' Clovis said, catching up and understanding.

'Right! Aw, you're a bright little feller, you sure are. Ain't he a bright feller, Theodore? Ain't he sweet?'

It was all standing right there in front of Clovis. The chance to be rich and famous—and to let the two old goats off besides. More than he had ever dreamed of: everything.

'All right?' the old man chuckled, taking a step toward him, gun in hand. 'Okay, sonny?'

Clovis hesitated, torn between desires. He wanted to be a hero. The money would mean so much, with Dad still away. . . .

'Here!' the old man grinned. 'Here, sonny! We'll do it jus' like I said, okay? Here you are, little buddy!'

And he thrust the rusty revolver into Clovis's hand.

Then he turned and started scooping up coins.

The actions somehow decided for Clovis.

'No,' he said huskily.

The old man turned. 'Huh?'

'You can . . . go,' Clovis said, struggling with himself. 'But you can't take no money.'

'Aw! Look, sonny—'

'*No!*' Clovis said shrilly. 'And you better git outta here right now, before I change my dadburned mind!'

The old man on the horse croaked, 'We gotta have

some money! I need medical attention, boy! I want a new hoss with a fancy saddle.'

'Get moving,' Clovis ordered. With difficulty, he managed to heel back the hammer of the old gun.

The other old man took a step toward him. 'You little— !'

Clovis swung the gun around to aim at the old codger's belly. 'I'm tellin' you! You better go fast! I might change my stupid mind!'

The man on horseback urged, '*Rush* him, Amos!'

But Amos stared at the gun, and then his shoulders slumped. 'You'd *do* it, too, wouldn't you, boy?' he said softly.

'You better believe it,' Clovis said with more certainty than he felt.

Amos turned and limped to his horse, struggled into the saddle.

His partner bawled, 'Are we leavin' with *nothing*?'

'We're leaving with our skins, you idjit! Now *c'mon*!'

Clovis stood with his back to the sun-warmed brick wall and watched the two men turn their ragged mounts, walk them down the alley, and disappear into a side street.

Clovis took a deep breath and looked at all the gold around him on the ground.

He was, he told himself, the biggest fool that ever walked the earth.

Chapter Sixteen

'—and so I seen these two young guys there, an' when I run over, they took off, headin' north,' Clovis gasped in conclusion.

Standing in his office, Adam Bricker held the trembling boy in his arms. Bricker was too astonished to respond. Clovis's heart was going like a triphammer against Bricker's chest. He had been scared half to death.

The office door bust open and Billy Dean rushed in, hatless. 'It's the truth, Sheriff! Somebody was there! Gold coins all over the floor and the alley!'

'Get some men headed north,' Bricker ordered. 'Guard the bank. Find carpenter to help board things up. Have Tim Whitaker get over there and pick up all the money somehow.'

Dean nodded and rushed out again, slamming the door on the frenzied hole-digging and drinking taking place out in what had been the street.

Bricker had figured on scolding him, but he was tired and Clovis was exhausted and scared, and there was something else, too: Clovis radiated a certain feeling, something different. He had entered into the time of beginning young manhood.

'Okay,' Bricker said gruffly. 'We'll just forget about it.'

Clovis brightened with relief. 'Gee, thanks! I thought—'

The door burst open again and Adele hurried in. 'Sheriff! Sheriff! I heard Clovis—' She saw him. '*Clovis!*' With a glad cry, she grabbed the boy in her arms and began sobbing.

The door opened once more, and Colonel T. T. Clydesdale, looking somewhat the worse for wear, sauntered in. 'I understand, my good man, that the youthful hero is being interrogated.'

Behind the colonel was Enright, notebook in hand.

'Young man,' the colonel intoned, planting a hammy hand on Clovis's skinny shoulder, 'you may have saved this financial institution tragic loss . . . yes, tragic loss. Your efforts will not go unrewarded.'

Clovis stared at the colonel, his eyes like pie pans. 'Reward?'

Enright sat on the edge of Bricker's desk. 'I'd like to interview you, boy. For a story in the newspaper.'

'A story?' Clovis repeated in awe. 'In the newspaper? About *me*?'

Enright grinned and winked at Bricker. 'I think the readers will eat it up.'

'Indeed they will, sir,' the colonel pronounced, still massaging Clovis's shoulder. 'A feat of heroic wisdom for one so tender in years. I am reminded of one of my own experiences among the wild Indians of the north.' He fixed Adele with a bright eye.

'Yes,' Adele said breathlessly. 'And the reward—you're so kind, Colonel Clydesdale! I know Clovis didn't *expect* a reward.'

'A reward,' the colonel said. He coughed into his glove. 'Yes. Indeed. A reward. I should explain, my dear, that metaphorical usage—'

Bricker saw what was coming and cut in, 'Yeah, Colonel. Darned nice of you. Ought to make a nice item for the paper.' He glanced at Enright.

Enright picked it up at once, stifling a grin. 'Make a nice sidebar for the story of Clovis's adventure, Colonel. Yes indeed. How much did you say the reward was, so I can publish it correctly?'

Colonel Clydesdale lost some of his colour. He was trapped, and saw it. He pulled back from Clovis as if he had the plague. 'Yes. Well. Uh, the precise amount has not been determined. Uh—'

Bricker said, 'Fifty dollars would be a nice amount.'

'Yes, it would,' Enright said.

Clovis looked ecstatic and the colonel looked like the world had ended.

Adele whispered, 'Fifty *dollars*?'

'Of course,' Bricker added, 'that might be too much—'

'No,' the colonel gasped, then got his air back and recovered. 'No!—I would say—uh—fifty dollars—uh, yes. Uh—'

'*Gosh!*' Clovis yelped, beaming.

'That's a good story,' Enright said, scribbling.

'Yes,' the colonel muttered, looking wild-eyed. 'Uh, it should be pointed out, however, that I am momentarily short of funds, actual cash on hand, as it were—'

'You can draw it from the bank with no trouble at all,' Bricker said. 'Right?'

Everyone looked at the colonel.

He tried to speak, but no words came out.

Enright grinned. 'We can have a little ceremony. That will make a good part of the story, too. As soon as I interview the boy, Colonel, you'll give him the money. Right?'

'Right,' Colonel Clydesdale said, strangled. 'I uh . . . I depart from you now, my good friends.' He mustered a sick smile and patted Clovis on the head. 'I— uh—'

The door came open again. Billy Dean was back. 'I got 'em all moving, Sheriff.'

With a glad little cry, Adele ran across the room and threw herself into the startled deputy's arms. 'I've been so *worried* about you!'

'About *me?*' Dean choked again.

'Oh, Billy, I was so scared, honey! Oh darling—!' She kissed him soundly on the mouth and clung.

Chapter Seventeen

By Monday afternoon, Hopewell was back to as near normalcy as the town was likely to get for a long, long time.

Saturday night had been one to remember. Everyone within fifty miles, it seemed, had decided to tie one on in celebration of the bank robbery's failure. Bricker, dead on his feet, had gone on his rounds expecting the worst. Within minutes he imagined he had found it: two youthful waddies squaring off with knives in an alley.

Neither man was blooded yet, and Bricker moved through the dim light toward them, warning, 'You two are the ones who are going to get hurt, boys. Put down the steel.'

One of the kids, hardly sixteen, bared his teeth. 'Don't interfere, mister!'

Before Bricker could respond, three burly shapes pushed past him from behind, startling him badly. The three men—Stein, Criswell, and the baker—walked up to the two youths, grabbed them, wrestled for an instant, and disarmed them as if they had been doing things like that in dark alleys all their lives.

'Boy,' Criswell told the one kid softly, 'You don't *do*

stuff like that in Hopewell. We got law here; us citizens help our sheriff.'

And that had been the way things went. Every time Bricker saw trouble ahead, he had so much help he was falling over people.

Now, Monday afternoon, Colonel Clydesdale was preparing to take the afternoon train back East. It wasn't in yet, but its smoke stained the western horizon. The colonel was done up in his finest, a pale ivory suit with a tan stovepipe hat and flowered vest. His 'assistant' was with him, a stunning girl who kept throwing Bricker shyly inviting overtures with her lovely blue eyes. Mayor Steed was there, too, along with Tim Whitaker from the bank, U. S. Bagwell, and Harold Enright. They stood with Bricker on the platform beside the gleaming rails, waiting. It was hot.

'Yes, my friends,' the colonel garrumphed, twirling his cane, 'it has been most memorable. My friends in the Moose Lodge will thrill to the tale, and I assure you I plan personally to write various Eastern journalists, confident they will wish to enshrine this noble weekend in the records of the fourth estate.' He held out a pudgy hand. 'Sheriff, again allow me to congratulate you.'

Bricker shook his hand. It was soft and moist. 'Come back, Colonel.'

The colonel put his hand on Enright's shoulder. 'Remember my advice, sir. Tell the truth. Never exaggerate.' He added in a phony soto voice, 'And support Bricker in the election, he's going to beat any fool who runs against him.'

Enright grinned manfully. 'I'll remember, Colonel.'

The train chugged in, showering dirt and steam,

wheels clattering and banging and creaking—an engine, a service car, three passenger cars, and a caboose.

They trooped to the car. The colonel waved jauntily and bowed to let his girl step aboard. But just as she moved toward the steps, someone appeared in the doorway to leave the train here. A skinny man, gauntly pale, with huge, burning eyes. His suit was rumpled but clean, and he carried a carpetbag.

Bricker was jolted back a half-step with recognition. The man got down and walked directly toward him. 'Hello, Sheriff. I'm back.'

Bricker stared, incredulous and angry, at the tall man facing him.

Wintle pulled his hat off, revealing hair pasted to his head with perspiration and grease. 'I got the wires. I wasn't going to come back. Oh, I'm a bad man, Sheriff, I was going to run. But then I got to thinking . . . what kind of man would leave his children, dodge all his responsibilities, do a trick like that to a man like you? I knew I had to come back.'

Bricker stared at him. He had changed. Lost more weight, for one thing, and had gotten more pale and ragged. But these were not the real changes, not the significant ones. John Wintle was stone sober.

'I'm going to find a job,' Wintle told him huskily. 'I'm going to work. No more drinking. I'm going to raise my family.'

Bricker, staring at Wintle, took in these things only by way of background. He was wrestling with his own emotions. He had intended to do some punishing, and some bawling out. But Wintle, standing here now, was a changed—a chastened man.

Wintle said, 'My only worry is that the kids will know . . . will find out what I've been.'

'I'll talk to Enright,' Bricker said. 'He'll put in a story that makes it seem you really have been away on business. I'll spread the word elsewhere. The kids don't have to know.'

'The kids,' Wintle said, colour touching his face and his eyes coming alive. 'Can I please see them?'

Bricker clapped him on the back. 'Go.'

Wintle turned and hurried off, and Bricker turned to watch him.

Enright came over. 'Was that *Wintle*?'

'Yes,' Bricker said. 'Listen. I have something I want to explain to you.'

Helen Jefferson met him at her door with pleased surprise. 'Come in!'

Bricker stepped into her small living room, his hat in hand.

'Let me take your hat,' Helen said.

Bricker, who had had it clutched in his hands, gave it to her. She walked demurely to a table and placed it there, then turned and looked at him with a sweet, amused smile.

'What's so funny?' Bricker growled.

'You look so very, very nice, Adam.'

Bricker looked down at himself. 'Well, I don't wear my Sunday suit very often.'

She gestured him to the sofa, and sat beside him, her hands in her lap. 'And it isn't even Sunday. What *is* the occasion?'

'Well,' Bricker said, so nervous he thought he would

faint, 'I thought I'd tell you about Wintle getting back. And all that.' Which was a lie, of course.

'I've heard about it,' Helen told him softly, watching his eyes.

'Not from me,' Bricker grunted. 'But if you don't want to hear—'

She put her hand on his knee, staying his impulsive movement toward leaving. 'No! I mean, I want to hear it, from you.'

'Yeah,' Bricker muttered, more nervous than ever. He looked around.

'Can I give you some tea?' Helen asked, watching him again.

'I better go,' Bricker said. He lurched to his feet.

'I heard you'll collect a reward for several of the men you captured,' Helen said.

'Yeah,' Bricker grunted. 'Bobby Wintle has that reward coming for Simon Frink, too.'

'And you'll be re-elected now,' Helen said, standing and facing him. She was very close, her eyes were very level, her lips were parted, and the sweet odours of jasmine and mint and woman came from her body.

'I expect so,' Bricker said. 'Well—'

'So you have a secure future now,' Helen said softly.

'Yeah. Well—'

'And you found, taking care of the Wintle children, that you've been lonely,' Helen persisted quietly.

'Yeah.' Where was his hat? He had to get *out* of here. He was suffocating. Hell, he had no nerve at all, he had no *right*.

'So you came to see me,' Helen said.

'Yeah,' Bricker said.

'You have a good job, you have some money in the bank, you're lonely, and you like children,' Helen summed up.

'Right. Hey, where's my hat? I'd better—'

'Darn you, Adam Bricker!' Helen flared, tears appearing by magic in her eyes. 'I've said practically all of it for you! Are you some kind of dunce or something?'

Bricker stared at her, and he was in such a panic now that he was practically pulling a Doreen act. Helen was so lovely, so desirable, so much the perfect woman, and he was so scared, so petrified, and choked. . . .

'Helen—' he said, strangled.

'Yes?' she breathed.

He couldn't say it.

'All right,' Helen whispered. 'I'll help you, Adam. I've tried, but I'll go ahead. I'll guess. You want to ask me to marry you. That's what you came here for.' She fixed him with bright, loving eyes.

Bricker stared at her, transfixed.

'Right?' she asked.

'Yes—'

'And you want to say you love me dearly, and you want to have children, and you'll take care of me?' Helen cried.

'Yes,' Bricker said, strangled.

Helen cried softly and then was suddenly in his arms, hugging him furiously. 'That's the sweetest proposal any woman ever had, you silly goose! Yes! Of course I'll marry you!'

THE FLYING SORCERERS

BY DAVID GERROLD AND LARRY NIVEN

SHOOGAR was absolutely livid – a natural state for any self-respecting witch-doctor . . .
But this time he had a reason. His territory had been invaded by a completely insane shaman who hadn't had the grace to announce himself and didn't even appear to know the common ground rules of the magicians' guild. And what's more, the idiot dared to practice witchcraft without having first made his gift to the local witch-doctor, who happened to be the mighty Shoogar . . .

In an absolute fury Shoogar prepared his most ghastly spells to drive the foreigner away . . . little did he know that the stranger had quite a few ghastly spells of his own to fall back on . . .

o 552 09907 4   6op

DANDELION WINE BY RAY BRADBURY

is set in the strange world of Green Town, Illinois, where there was a junkman who saved lives; a pair of shoes that could make you run as fast as a deer; a human time machine; a wax witch that could tell real fortunes; and a man who almost destroyed happiness by building a happiness machine. But there was also a twelve-year-old boy named Douglas Spaulding, who found himself very much at home in this extraordinary world . . .

o 552 09882 5   45p

A SELECTED LIST OF CORGI WESTERNS
FOR YOUR READING PLEASURE

J. T. EDSON

☐ 07991 X	THE HOODED RIDERS No. 21		J. T. Edson 45p
☐ 08011 X	THE BULL WHIP BREED No. 22		J. T. Edson 45p
☐ 08017 9	THE COLT AND THE SABRE No. 26		J. T. Edson 45p
☐ 08132 9	THE SMALL TEXAN No. 36		J. T. Edson 35p
☐ 08241 4	THE FORTUNE HUNTERS No. 47		J. T. Edson 40p
☐ 08279 1	SIDEWINDER No. 52		J. T. Edson 40p
☐ 08706 8	SLIP GUN No. 65		J. T. Edson 40p
☐ 08783 1	HELL IN THE PALO DURO No. 66		J. T. Edson 40p
☐ 09650 4	YOUNG OLE DEVIL No. 76		J. T. Edson 40p
☐ 09905 8	GET URREA No. 77		J. T. Edson 40p

LOUIS L'AMOUR

☐ 09849 3	SACKETT'S LAND		Louis L'Amour 40p
☐ 09354 8	LANDO		Louis L'Amour 40p
☐ 09353 X	RADIGAN		Louis L'Amour 40p
☐ 09352 1	THE BURNING HILLS		Louis L'Amour 40p
☐ 09351 3	CONAGHER		Louis L'Amour 40p
☐ 09350 5	THE LONELY MEN		Louis L'Amour 40p
☐ 09343 2	DOWN THE LONG HILLS		Louis L'Amour 40p
☐ 08157 4	FALLON		Louis L'Amour 40p
☐ 07815 8	MATAGORDA		Louis L'Amour 40p

MORGAN KANE

☐ 09425 0	DUEL IN TOMBSTONE No. 23		Louis Masterson 35p
☐ 09467 6	TO THE DEATH, SENOR KANE! No. 24		Louis Masterson 35p
☐ 09764 0	BLOODY EARTH No. 28		Louis Masterson 30p
☐ 09794 2	NEW ORLEANS GAMBLE No. 29		Louis Masterson 30p
☐ 09877 9	APACHE BREAKOUT No. 30		Louis Masterson 35p

SUDDEN

☐ 09117 0	SUDDEN TAKES THE TRAIL		Oliver Strange 35p
☐ 09118 9	THE LAW O' THE LARIAT		Oliver Strange 35p
☐ 09063 8	SUDDEN – GOLDSEEKER		Oliver Strange 35p
☐ 08907 9	SUDDEN – TROUBLESHOOTER		Frederick H. Christian 35p
☐ 08813 7	SUDDEN AT BAY		Frederick H. Christian 30p

All these books are available at your bookseller or newsagent: or can be ordered direct from the publisher. Just tick the titles you want and fill in the form below.

CORGI BOOKS, Cash Sales Department, P.O. Box 11, Falmouth, Cornwall.

Please send cheque or postal order, no currency.
U.K. and Eire send 15p for first book plus 5p per copy for each additional book ordered to a maximum charge of 50p to cover the cost of postage and packing.
Overseas Customers and B.F.P.O. allow 20p for first book and 10p per copy for each additional book.

NAME (Block letters)..

ADDRESS ....

(OCT. 75) ....

While every effort is made to keep prices low, it is sometimes necessary to increase prices at short notice. Corgi Books reserve the right to show new retail prices on covers which may differ from those previously advertised in the text or elsewhere.